The Sell Sword and The Elf

Matthew Gage

Published by MG Books, 2025.

THE SELL SWORD AND THE ELF

First edition. March 27, 2025.

Copyright © 2025 Matthew Gage.

ISBN: 979-8230302643

Written by Matthew Gage.

Table of Contents

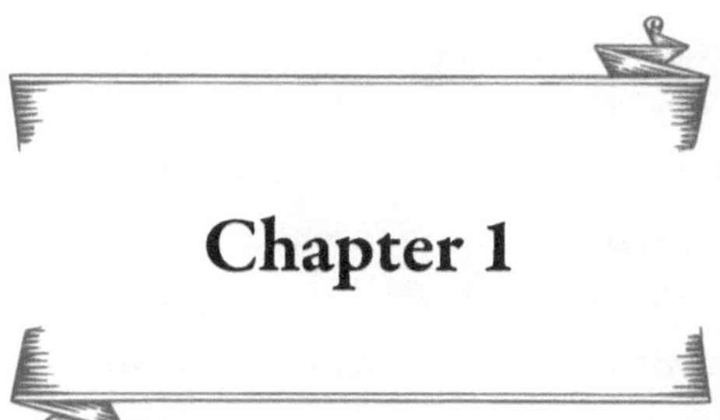

Chapter 1

The air hung heavy with the scent of ale, sweat, and simmering resentment as Nagar pushed through the crowded inn. His broad shoulders, encased in thick leather armor, parted the sea of patrons like a ship's prow cleaving through a storm. Heads turned, conversations faltered, and eyes, some curious, others wary, tracked his progress. He wasn't a man who relied on looks to command attention, but his presence was undeniable. His dark skin, rich as midnight and etched with the scars of countless battles, spoke of a life lived on the edge. Braided black hair, tight against his scalp, framed a face that was more functional than handsome – a blunt instrument honed for survival. But it was the great sword strapped across his back, its hilt peeking over his shoulder like a silent sentinel, that truly announced his arrival. Nagar wasn't alone. Beside him, a figure as contrasting as moonlight to his shadow moved with a grace that belied her deadly precision. Irma, his elf companion, her beige skin glowing with a subtle luminescence, her almond eyes holding an ancient wisdom beyond her years. Dark hair, cascading in a cascade reminiscent of silk, framed her face, accentuating the delicate points of her ears, a clear mark of her elven heritage. Her form, slender and lithe, was clad in tight leather breeches that hugged her curves, a shapely breastplate molded to her torso, and bracers that hinted at the strength beneath her delicate frame. A bow, its wood polished to a warm sheen, was slung across her back, and a dagger, its blade gleaming with a dangerous edge, hung at her hip. She was a vision of lethal beauty, a whisper of death in a world that often underestimated her kind.

The inn, a haven for travelers and mercenaries alike, buzzed with the usual mix of laughter, arguments, and the clatter of tankards. But as Irma entered, the atmosphere shifted. Whispers followed her like shadows, laced with prejudice and suspicion. Elves, though not unheard of in these parts, were often viewed with distrust, considered second-class citizens in a world dominated by humans. The shopkeeper, a burly man with a greasy smile and a paunch that strained against his apron, emerged from behind the bar, his eyes narrowing at Irma's pointed ears. "Elf, eh?" he grunted, his voice dripping with condescension. "Best wait outside. We don't cater to your kind in here."

Nagar's hand, calloused and scarred, shot out, resting possessively on Irma's shoulder. His voice, deep and gravelly, cut through the tension like a blade through silk. "She's with me. Cross her, and you cross me."

The shopkeeper's smirk faltered, replaced by a flicker of uncertainty. He knew Nagar, knew his reputation as a sell-sword, a man who didn't shy away from violence. The great sword on his back wasn't just for show. "Alright, alright," the shopkeeper muttered, taking a step back, his hands raised in a placating gesture. "No need to get worked up. Just... keep her under control, will ya?"

Nagar's gaze, cold and unflinching, held the shopkeeper's for a moment longer before he turned his attention to the reason they were here. A man, a merchant by the look of his fine clothes, sat hunched over a table in the corner, his eyes darting nervously between Nagar and Irma.

"Debt's due, merchant," Nagar said, his voice low and dangerous. "Time to pay up."

The merchant, a slimy man with a face like a weasel, paled. "I... I don't have it all yet. Give me a few more days, please."

Nagar's patience, never his strongest suit, snapped. "You had your chance. Now you have a choice: pay, or face the consequences." "Or else?" the merchant sneered, a desperate edge creeping into his voice. "What are you going to do? Kill me?"

A deadly silence descended upon the inn. Nagar's hand drifted towards the hilt of his sword, his fingers curling around it with a familiarity born of countless battles. Irma, ever vigilant, nocked an arrow, her bowstring humming with tension.

The merchant, realizing his mistake too late, scrambled to his feet, his chair clattering to the floor. "Wait! Wait! I'll pay, I'll pay!" He fumbled with his purse, pulling out a handful of coins, his hands trembling.

Nagar snatched the coins, his eyes never leaving the merchant's face. "Not enough," he growled.

Panic flashed in the merchant's eyes. He lunged for a dagger hidden beneath his cloak, but Irma's arrow was faster. It whistled through the air, embedding itself in the table mere inches from the merchant's hand. He froze, his eyes widening in terror. "Last chance," Nagar said, his voice devoid of emotion.

The merchant, defeated, slumped back into his chair, his shoulders sagging. "Take it all," he whispered, pushing his entire purse across the table.

Nagar scooped up the purse, the weight of the coins a satisfying confirmation of a job well done. He turned to Irma, a faint smile playing on his lips. "Let's go."

As they made their way towards the door, the inn erupted into a cacophony of whispers and pointed fingers. Nagar, his gaze sweeping the room, stopped abruptly. "Anyone else want to try their luck?" he challenged, his voice carrying a dangerous edge.

The room fell silent. No one met his gaze.

With a nod of satisfaction, Nagar and Irma stepped out into the bustling streets of the city of Green Kingdom. The sun, a fiery orb hanging low in the afternoon sky, cast long shadows across the cobblestones. Vendors hawked their wares, the scent of roasted meat and spices mingling with the tang of sweat and dust.

"The broker said that the man only owed twelve gold coins. Why did you take twenty?" Irma asked

Nagar smirked, "what the broker doesn't know, ain't going to kill him. We're only getting paid two coins each for this bounty. I figured the rest of his debt is only a finder's fee."

Irma laughed, "and this is why I've stuck around you for so long. Always thinking ahead."

"Are you sure it wasn't my good looks?"

Irma laughed. "Please, you humans are disgusting." She mocked with a coy smile.

"Sure." Nagar winked. "I've known you for over ten years. You always had a thing for humans."

"No, I only like you because you've gotten me paid through the years. Other than that, I could care less. I'm here for the money."

"Aw, you're breaking my heart."

"Whatever." She giggled. "Where's my cut?"

Nagar sorted through the coin purse and tossed her six coins.

"You gave me too much. An even cut would've been five."

"Keep it." He winked.

"Thanks." Irma grinned as she followed him through the city.

As they walked, Nagar, his senses always alert, caught snippets of conversations as they walked. Whispers of a recent attack in the city square by a group of ruthless orcs, a princess kidnapped by the orcs, and a king desperate for her return. His lips curled into a predatory grin. This was the kind of opportunity he lived for – a chance for riches, for glory, and perhaps, just perhaps, a chance to make a name for himself beyond the shadows of the mercenary world. "Irma," he said, his voice low, "we might have just found our next job."

Irma, her eyes scanning the crowd, nodded. "Orcs, you say? That could be tricky. They're not known for their hospitality."

"Tricky is my middle name," Nagar replied with a wink. "Besides, the king's offering a handsome reward. And who knows, maybe we'll even get to play hero for a change."

Their path led them towards the city square, where a crowd had gathered around a group of knights. The scene looked to be frantic as several slain bodies laid about, including knights and dead orcs. Servants helped clean up the bodies, while knights shouted orders at various soldiers running about. Near a nearby empty stall, several knights had to hold back King Hector, a burly man with a long beard, as he shouted to let him go find his daughter. Nagar, his ears attuned to the buzz of conversation, overheard snippets of the discussion from the other sell swords that had gathered about.

"...Princess Vanessa has been taken by orcs..."

"...King Hector's offering riches beyond measure..."

"...title of prince to whoever brings her back..."

Nagar's grin widened. This was better than he'd hoped. He pushed through the crowd, Irma close behind, until they reached the front.

A knight, his armor gleaming in the sunlight, was addressing the assembled crowd. "King Hector is desperate for his daughter, Princess Vanessa's safe return. He has promised riches beyond your wildest dreams, and the hand of the princess herself, to the man who brings her back."

A murmur of excitement rippled through the crowd. Nagar, his eyes narrowing, scanned the faces of the knights. He recognized a few — veterans of countless battles, their faces etched with the same hardness he saw in the mirror. "Where was she taken?" Nagar called out, his voice cutting through the chatter.

The knight turned, his gaze assessing Nagar from head to toe. "We believe the orcs took her to their camp in the Margo Mountains."

Nagar exchanged a glance with Irma. The Margo Mountains were a treacherous range, known for their harsh terrain and the fierce orc tribes that called them home. But something about the knight's certainty nagged at him.

As the crowd began to disperse, Nagar spotted a small object on the ground, partially hidden by a clump of grass. He bent down, picking it up. It was a trinket, a carved wooden figurine of a bull, its features crude but unmistakable.

"This isn't from the Margo orcs," Nagar said, turning the figurine over in his hand. "This is Wontrui clan. I've seen their craftsmanship before."

The knight, his brow furrowing, snatched the figurine from Nagar's hand. "Are you sure? It could be from any clan."

"I'm sure," Nagar said, his voice firm. "The Wontrui have distinct art style. This is theirs."

The knight, clearly skeptical, turned to his companions. "We're heading to the Margo camp. That's where the closest orc tribe is. It wouldn't make sense for the Wontrui tribe to travel all this way."

Nagar, his eyes locking with Irma's, knew they had to follow their own path. The Wontrui clan, known for their cunning and brutality, were a different breed altogether. If the princess was with them, the rescue mission would be far more dangerous than anyone anticipated. "Come on, Irma," Nagar said, turning away from the crowd. "We've got a princess to save, and a king's reward to claim."

As they disappeared into the bustling streets of Green Kingdom, the weight of their decision hung heavy in the air. The Wontrui village awaited, along with a labyrinth of danger and uncertainty. But for Nagar and Irma, the promise of adventure, riches, and perhaps even a chance to prove themselves as more than just sell-swords, was irresistible. The fate of the princess, and their own, now lay intertwined in the heart of the treacherous mountains, where the Wontrui tribe reigned supreme.

Chapter 2

After a day's ride, the two sell swords enjoyed a well-deserved rest at their makeshift camp. The fire crackled between them, its dancing flames casting long shadows across the campsite. Nagar and Irma sat side by side, the warmth of the blaze a welcome contrast to the cool night air. The forest around them was alive with the whispers of nocturnal creatures, the occasional hoot of an owl or the distant howl of a wolf punctuating the silence. Their horses grazed nearby, tethered to a low-hanging branch, their soft nickers a comforting background to the conversation unfolding.

Nagar leaned back on his elbows; his dark weathered face illuminated by the firelight. His eyes, sharp and calculating, held a hint of amusement as he regarded Irma and their previous conversation during their travels.

"So, if I marry the princess and become king, you'd think I'd make a terrible ruler, do you?" he asked, his voice laced with a mixture of challenge and curiosity.

Irma, her delicate features softened by the flickering light, shrugged. Her pointed ears twitched slightly, a subtle gesture that betrayed her elven heritage. "I didn't say that," she replied, her voice light and tinkling, like wind chimes in a gentle breeze. "I just can't picture you sitting on a throne, issuing decrees and worrying about the welfare of your subjects."

Nagar let out a hearty laugh, the sound echoing through the trees. "And why's that? Because I'm a sell-sword, a mercenary with no loyalty beyond the gold in my purse?"

Irma tilted her head, her delicate almond shaped eyes sparkling with mischief. "Well, it's not exactly the résumé of a future monarch, is it?"

He chuckled, a deep, rumbling sound that seemed to come from his very core. "True enough. But tell me, Irma, what would you do if you were queen? Would you rule with an iron fist, or would you be a benevolent sovereign, beloved by your people?"

She considered his question for a moment, her gaze drifting into the flames as if searching for the answer within their dancing embers. "I don't think it's in the cards for us elves," she said finally, her voice quiet and reflective. "All my life, and the one before it, all I've ever heard about is a human king. We're lucky we're not in bonds anymore, but the idea of a monarch who isn't human... it's not something I've ever given much thought to."

Nagar's expression softened, his usual air of cynicism giving way to a rare moment of sincerity. "You've lived through a lot, haven't you? Seen things that no one should have to see."

Irma's eyes met his, her gaze steady and unflinching. "We all have our scars, Nagar. Yours are just more visible than mine."

He grunted, a noncommittal sound that acknowledged her words without fully agreeing with them. "Maybe," he conceded. "But tell me, if you could have anything in the world, what would it be? Forget about kings and queens for a moment. What's your heart's desire?"

Irma's lips curved into a small, secretive smile. "Freedom," she said simply. "The freedom to live my life as I choose, without the constraints of tradition or expectation. To roam the forests, to feel the wind in my hair, and to know that I'm not bound by the chains of the past."

Nagar's eyes narrowed, his gaze intense and probing. "And what about love? Does it have no place in your ideal world?"

She laughed, a light, musical sound that seemed to chase away the shadows. "Love is a complicated thing, Nagar. It's not something that can be easily defined or contained. It's like trying to capture the wind in your hands."

"And yet," he persisted, his voice low and persuasive, "you've felt it, haven't you? The pull of it, the ache of it?"

Irma's smile faded, replaced by a look of wistfulness. "Perhaps," she admitted. "But love is a luxury, Nagar. One that often comes with a price."

He leaned forward, his elbows resting on his knees as he regarded her intently. "And what about us? Where do we fit into this grand scheme of yours?"

She met his gaze, her eyes shining with a mixture of emotions. "You and I, Nagar... we're kindred spirits. We've both seen the darkness, felt the weight of the world on our shoulders. But together, we're stronger. We balance each other out."

Nagar's lips twisted into a wry smile. "So, you're saying I'm the best thing you've ever had in your two-hundred-year lifespan?"

Irma laughed, the sound echoing through the trees. "Something like that. In my two hundred and twenty years, I've never fought along someone like you. Not only do you keep a smile on my face, but you are also wise beyond your years, and brave. We make a good team, you and me. You're the brute force, the raw power, while I'm the finesse, the subtlety. Together, we're a force to be reckoned with."

He grinned, his eyes glinting with amusement. "I'll take that as a compliment. But tell me, Irma, do you ever think about settling down? Putting down roots, finding a place to call your own?"

She shook her head, her silk like black hair cascading over her shoulders like a waterfall. "I'm a wanderer, Nagar. I will outlive you and many others. The open road is my home, the stars my compass. I can't imagine being tied down to one place. Nor..." she breathed her eyes connecting to him as if there was more to the story, "...one person.

What about you? I can't see being tied down. If you did get married, what would all the prostitutes in Green Kingdom do? They will all go broke without your coin." She teased.

Nagar's expression turned playful, his eyes twinkling with mischief. "So, you're saying the brothels would run dry if I ever got married?"

Irma chuckled, her eyes sparkling with laughter. "I didn't say that. But let's just say I can't see you settling down with one woman. You've got a reputation to uphold, after all."

He smirked, leaning back on his elbows. "Hey, now, you are one to judge, I've seen how you spend your coin when we're together at the brothels. You've got a soft spot for humans. I'm sure in my absence you'd keep them open."

Irma's cheeks flushed, a delicate pink hue that contrasted with her pale skin. "I may have a fondness for your kind," she admitted, her voice teasing. "But it's not just about the coin, Nagar. It's about the experience, the thrill of the moment."

"And what about me?" he asked, his voice low and seductive. "Do I thrill you, Irma?"

She met his gaze, her eyes shining with a mixture of emotions. "You challenge me, Nagar. You push me to be better, to be stronger. And yes, there are times when you thrill me beyond measure."

The air between them seemed to crackle with tension, the unspoken words hanging heavy in the silence. Nagar's hand reached out, his fingers brushing against hers in a gesture that was both tender and tentative.

"So, you're seriously considering giving up your ways for marriage?" Irma asked, her voice soft and curious. "If it's with the right partner, yes," Nagar admitted, his tone surprisingly sincere. "I would."

Their conversation was interrupted by the sound of snapping twigs, the noise echoing through the forest like a warning shot. Nagar's hand instinctively went to the hilt of his great sword, his body tensing as he scanned the darkness for any sign of danger.

Irma's bow was already in her hand, her fingers nocking an arrow with a speed and precision that spoke of years of practice. Her eyes narrowed; her gaze fixed on the shadows as she waited for the threat to reveal itself.

The underbrush rustled, the sound growing louder as a group of figures emerged from the trees. Nagar's eyes widened as he recognized the distinctive features of the orcs, their green skin and tusks glinting in the firelight.

"A scouting party," he muttered, his voice low and dangerous. "We must have wandered into their territory."

Irma's arrow was already aimed, her finger resting on her cheek as she waited for the signal to attack. The orcs, sensing their presence, let out a series of guttural cries, their voices rising in a chorus of aggression.

Nagar's sword was out in an instant, the steel glinting in the firelight as he stepped forward to meet the threat. "Stay behind me, Irma," he ordered, his voice firm and commanding. "I'll handle this."

But Irma was already moving, her bow singing as she loosed a volley of arrows into the advancing ranks. The orcs roared in anger, their charges becoming more frantic as they sought to close the distance.

The fight was brief but brutal, a chaotic blur of steel and flesh as Nagar and Irma fought back-to-back against the onslaught. Nagar's sword flashed in the darkness, each strike finding its mark as he carved a path through the enemy.

Irma's arrows flew true, each one finding its target with unerring accuracy. The orcs fell back, their cries of pain and anger filling the air as they sought to regroup and relaunch their attack.

But it was too late. Nagar and Irma had gained the upper hand, their coordinated assault leaving the orcs reeling. With a final, mighty blow, Nagar dispatched the last of their attackers, his sword sinking deep into the chest of the lead orc.

The forest fell silent, the only sound the heavy breathing of the two companions as they stood amidst the carnage. Nagar's chest heaved, his body slick with sweat as he turned to regard Irma.

"That was too close," he said, his voice rough and shaken. "We need to move, find a safer place to camp."

Irma nodded, her eyes scanning the surroundings as she sought to ensure their safety. "Agreed. But first..." She moved to Nagar's side, her hands reaching out to examine the wound he had sustained during the fight.

"It's just a flesh wound," he grunted, waving off her concern. "I've had worse."

"Nonsense," she replied, her voice firm and insistent. "You'll bleed out if I don't tend to it."

Nagar opened his mouth to protest, but Irma's hands were already weaving a healing charm, her fingers dancing in the air as she summoned the ancient magic of her people. The air around them seemed to shimmer, the very fabric of reality bending to her will.

"Irma, don't," Nagar protested, his voice laced with concern. "You know the cost of such magic. It saps away your life-force, leaves you weakened and vulnerable."

But Irma ignored him, her eyes fixed on the wound as she channeled her power into the healing spell. "Elves live for a thousand years," she said softly, her voice barely audible over the whispering wind. "Yes, using this spell takes away a few years, but let's face it, I've got a few to spare."

The charm took effect, the wound closing with a speed that defied explanation. Nagar's pain eased, the tension draining from his body as the magic worked its wonders.

He smirked, his eyes glinting with amusement as he regarded Irma. "Admit it, Irma. You can't live your life without me."

Irma's hands fell to her sides, her eyes meeting his in a gaze that was both tender and challenging. "Perhaps," she conceded, her voice soft and teasing. "But it's not just about you, Nagar. It's about us, about the bond we share."

The fire crackled between them, its flames casting a warm glow over the campsite. The forest was quiet now, the only sound the soft rustling of leaves as the wind whispered through the trees.

Nagar's hand reached out, his fingers brushing against Irma's in a gesture that was both tender and tentative. "We make a good team, you and I," he said, his voice low and sincere. "A force to be reckoned with."

Irma's smile was soft, her eyes shining with a mixture of emotions. "We do," she agreed. "And together, we can face whatever challenges lie ahead."

The night deepened around them, the stars twinkling like diamonds in the velvet sky. The world was full of wonder and magic, a tapestry of adventure and mystery that awaited their discovery.

And as they sat together, side by side, the unspoken bond between them grew stronger, a connection that transcended words and defied explanation. They were kindred spirits, bound by a shared history and a common purpose.

The future was uncertain, a blank canvas waiting to be filled. But together, Nagar and Irma would face it head-on, their courage and determination a beacon of hope in a world filled with darkness and danger.

As the fire burned low, casting long shadows across the campsite, they shared a smile, the unspoken understanding between them a promise of things to come. The road ahead would be long and arduous, but with each other by their side, they would overcome any obstacle, conquer any challenge.

For in each other, they had found a home, a sense of belonging that transcended the boundaries of race and culture. They were partners, companions, and friends, bound by a love that was as strong as it was unspoken.

And as they prepared to face the challenges of the coming day, they knew that together, they could achieve anything. The world was theirs to explore, to conquer, and to shape according to their own desires.

The night wore on, the silence broken only by the occasional crackle of the fire or the distant call of a nocturnal creature. Nagar and Irma sat in comfortable silence, their thoughts turning to the journey ahead and the mysteries that awaited them.

Chapter 3

The fire crackled between them, its orange glow casting long shadows across the forest floor. Nagar and Irma sat side by side, the warmth of the flames a stark contrast to the chill that had settled in Irma's demeanor. Earlier that day, they had fought their way through another group of orc scouts, their blades singing a brutal symphony as they clashed with the brutish creatures. The battle had been fierce, but Nagar and Irma moved as one, their years of partnership evident in every strike and parry. After the dust settled, they had captured one of the orcs, a snarling beast with a face twisted in hatred. Through broken words and guttural growls, the orc had revealed that they were getting closer to their destination.

Nagar had turned to Irma, his expression grim but determined. "We're gaining on them. They can't be more than a day's ride away. We'll rescue Princess Vanessa, get our riches and..."

"you'll marry the princess..." Irma interrupted.

"Yes." His voice was steady, but Irma noticed a flicker of something in his eyes—a weight he carried but never spoke of. She nodded, her own resolve hardening, but the thought of what lay ahead gnawed at her.

Now, as they sat by the fire, Irma's usual lively spirit was conspicuously absent. Her eyes were distant, her hands clasped tightly in her lap. Nagar noticed her quietness, the way she stared into the flames as if searching for answers. "What's wrong?" he asked, his voice soft, almost hesitant.

She shook her head, her jet-black hair catching the firelight, and insisted it was nothing. But Nagar had never seen her so upset. He reached out, his calloused hand gripping her shoulders gently but firmly. "Tell me. What is it?"

Irma's breath hitched, and for a moment, she fought the tears threatening to spill over. But the dam broke, and she turned to him, her eyes glistening with unshed tears. "I love you, Nagar," she admitted, the words tumbling out in a rush.

"What?" He gawked caught off guard by her confession. "After all this time, why haven't you told me?"

"I don't know. I'm afraid. Then you saying you'd marry Princess Vanessa made me realize I'll never get to see you again."

The air between them seemed to thicken, heavy with unspoken truths. Nagar's heart clenched, and without hesitation, he pulled her close, his lips crashing against hers. Fuck the princess, fuck the mission—in that moment, there was only her.

Their kiss was desperate, hungry, as if they could devour each other whole. Irma's hands tangled in his hair, pulling him closer, while Nagar's arms wrapped around her, holding her as if she might disappear. The fire crackled behind them, its warmth a distant echo as their bodies pressed together, heat radiating from their skin.

Nagar broke the kiss, his breath ragged as he trailed kisses along her jawline, down her neck. Irma shivered, her head falling back, exposing the delicate curve of her throat. "Nagar," she murmured, her voice trembling. "I want this. Please."

He didn't need to be told twice. With a growl, he stood, lifting her effortlessly into his arms. She wrapped her legs around his waist, her hands clutching at his shoulders as he carried her to a soft patch of earth near the warmth of the firelight. The ground was cool beneath them, but the heat of their desire burned hotter.

Nagar laid her down gently, his eyes never leaving hers. He shed his leather armor, the pieces clattering to the ground, and then helped her out of her armor, baring her petite body to the night air. He smiled admiring her beige skin in the firelight, her breasts small and perfect, her dark nipples were tight buds that pebbled under his gaze, and at her were apex was a soft patch of hair. He leaned down, taking her soft breast into his mouth, suckling gently as she arched her back with a soft moan.

Irma's hands roamed over his dark-skinned chest, tracing the scars that mapped his life as a sell-sword.

"You're so beautiful," he murmured against her skin, his lips moving down her stomach, pausing to nip at her navel. She squirmed, her breath quickening, her hips lifting in silent invitation.

Her body was a work of art, every curve and line a testament to her elven grace. He paused, drinking her in, before trailing kisses down her thighs, his beard scratching her sensitive skin.

His breath was warm against her sensitive skin as he positioned himself between her thighs. Her body arched slightly in anticipation, her fingers tangling in his dreadlocks as he gently parted her legs. With deliberate slowness, he kissed around her entrance, licking up the juices leaking from her, his lips soft and teasing, sending shivers through her.

When he reached his destination, he paused, his breath ghosting over her most intimate place, making her squirm with need. Then, with a slow, deliberate lick, he began to eat her out, his tongue tracing patterns that made her gasp and moan. He took his time, savoring her, his hands resting gently on her hips to hold her steady as he explored every inch of her with his mouth.

She moaned louder, her body tensing as pleasure built within her. He hummed against her, the vibration adding a new layer of sensation that made her cry out. His tongue was relentless, firm yet gentle, pushing her closer and closer to the edge. She dug her fingers into his scalp, urging him on, her hips lifting slightly to meet his mouth.

He smiled against her, the sensation sending another wave of pleasure through her. He knew exactly what he was doing, and he was determined to make her lose herself in the moment. His lips and tongue worked in perfect harmony, his rhythm steady and intoxicating. She felt her climax building, a tight coil of tension deep within her, ready to snap.

With one final, deliberate stroke of his tongue, he pushed her over the edge. She cried out, her body arching off the bed as her orgasm washed over her, waves of pleasure crashing through her. He didn't stop, his mouth moving in time with her tremors, milking every last drop of sensation from her.

When she finally came down, he kissed her softly one last time before lifting his head, his eyes meeting hers with a satisfied smile. She was breathless, her body still buzzing with the aftermath of her release, and she pulled him up to her, kissing him deeply, tasting herself on his lips. He had given her exactly what she needed, and she couldn't wait to return the favor.

"Nagar," she whispered, her voice thick with need. "Please. I need you."

He looked up at her, his eyes dark with desire, and slowly rose to his knees. He shed his own breeches, his black cock jutting proudly, thick and flushed. Irma's eyes widened at the sight, her lips parting in anticipation.

She reached for him, her hands guiding him to her entrance. But before he could enter her, she shifted, straddling him, her hands on his chest for balance. "I want to ride you," she said, her voice steady despite the tremor in her hands.

Nagar's breath caught as she lowered herself onto him, her warmth enveloping him in a tight, wet heat. She gasped, her head falling back as she took him in fully, her body adjusting to his size. He groaned, his hands moving to her hips, guiding her as she began to move.

Irma's hips swayed in a slow, rhythmic motion, her breasts bouncing with each thrust. Nagar watched her, mesmerized, his hands roaming over her body, cupping her face, tracing the curve of her waist. "You're so fucking beautiful," he growled, his voice rough with need.

She leaned down, her lips brushing his as she moved, their kisses deep and passionate. Nagar's hands moved to her ass, squeezing the firm flesh as he thrust upward, meeting her rhythm. The sound of their bodies slapping together filled the air, mingling with their moans and the crackle of the fire.

"Harder," she begged, her voice desperate. "Fuck me harder, Nagar."

He obliged, his hands gripping her hips tightly as he drove into her with increasing force. The ground beneath them shifted with each thrust, the world narrowing to the sensation of her body surrounding his, the heat of her skin against his.

"You feel so good," he groaned, his voice thick with desire. "So, fucking tight."

Irma's eyes fluttered closed as she rode him, her body trembling on the edge of release. "I'm close," she panted, her voice a whisper. "Don't stop."

Nagar pulled out of her, and she cried out begging for more. He kissed her and whispered in her ear, "Get on all fours..."

A naughty smile spread on her face as she assumed the position. Nagar stroked his black cock, groaning as he lubed up his cock with her lingering juices on his cock. He smacked her small tight ass and then slipped inside her. He moaned feeling her tightness and held her hips, plowing into her. He thrust into her with abandon, his hips snapping as he buried himself deep inside her. His dark fingers melted into her soft beige ass and gripped her tightly. He was hypnotized by the sway of her ass. He loved the way it jiggled every time his body crashed into hers.

"Cum for me," he commanded, his voice a low growl. "Let me feel you fall apart."

She obeyed, arching her back as she climaxed, her walls clenching around him in waves of pleasure. "Nagar," she cried, her voice breaking. "I'm cumming"

"That's it, let go."

When she was through, she moaned, "I want you to cum inside me."

He hesitated, just for a moment, the weight of her words settling over him. But then he surrendered, his release building like a storm. "Fuck," he groaned, his voice a ragged whisper as he spilled into her, his body shuddering with the force of it.

Afterward, they lay on the ground, panting, their bodies still entwined. The fire crackled nearby, its warmth a distant comfort as the heat of their passion faded. But as their hearts slowed, Irma's tears returned, slipping silently down her cheeks.

She pushed herself up, wiping her face with the back of her hand, and stood, her back rigid. "I can't be with you," she murmured, her voice breaking. "Not like this."

Nagar sat up, his chest heaving, his heart heavy with the knowledge that nothing would ever be the same. "Irma—"

She held up a hand, cutting him off. "Just let me sleep," she said, her voice hollow. She turned and walked away, her footsteps quiet on the forest floor, leaving Nagar alone with the dying fire and the weight of their unspoken future.

He watched her go, his heart aching, knowing that the rescue of the princess was no longer just a mission—it was a choice that would define the rest of their lives. And as the fire flickered, casting long shadows into the night, Nagar wondered if he could ever truly choose between duty and desire.

Chapter 4

The morning sun cast a pale, golden light over the desolate landscape, its rays barely piercing the thick canopy of the forest that surrounded Nagar and Irma's campsite. Nagar groaned as he stirred, his body stiff from the cold, hard ground. He blinked, his vision slowly adjusting to the dim light filtering through the trees. Beside him, the remnants of their makeshift fire smoldered, the embers barely glowing. Irma stood a few feet away, her back straight, her almond eyes sharp and narrowed. She was already dressed in her leather armor, her jet-black hair meticulously brushed, as if the raw, passionate night they had shared had never happened.

Nagar pushed himself up, his muscles protesting against the effort. He cleared his throat, attempting to break the tension that hung heavy in the air. "Irma," he began, his voice rough with sleep and emotion, "about last night—"

She cut him off with a cold, distant tone, her words like a blade slicing through the fragile moment. "It was a mistake. Once we save the princess, I'll take my share of the reward, and you'll never have to see me again."

Nagar shook his head, his heart aching. "That's not true, Irma. You know it's not—"

"We need to move," she interrupted, turning away from him. Her back was rigid, her shoulders tense. "If we don't catch up soon, we'll lose them for good."

The weight of her words pressed down on him, heavy and unrelenting. Nagar sighed, running a hand through his tousled dreadlocks. He knew Irma was trying to protect herself, to erect walls around her heart, but he couldn't let her push him away so easily. Not after what they had shared.

They mounted their horses in silence, the only sounds the soft crunch of leaves and the occasional rustle of the forest. The air between them was thick with unspoken words, with emotions neither of them knew how to articulate. Nagar glanced at Irma as they rode, her profile sharp against the morning light. Her jaw was set, her eyes fixed on the path ahead, as if she could outrun the feelings that lingered between them.

Hours passed, the forest giving way to a bleak, open plain. In the distance, the crude structures of the orc village loomed like a nightmare made real. Nagar's stomach tightened as they approached, the stench of smoke and decay reaching them long before they arrived. This was it. The moment they had been preparing for. The moment that would determine the fate of the princess—and perhaps their own.

But before they could act, a horde of orcs emerged from the village, their guttural roars filling the air. Nagar's heart sank as he realized they were outnumbered, outmatched. "Irma," he shouted, urging his horse forward, "we need to fall back!"

But Irma didn't retreat. Instead, she charged into the fray, her bow drawn, her arrows flying with deadly precision. Nagar followed, his sword flashing in the sunlight as he fought with a desperation born of fear and determination. The battle was chaotic, a blur of steel and blood, and for a moment, Nagar thought they might prevail.

Then, in an instant, everything changed.

A massive orc, wielding a war hammer, swung at Irma. She dodged, but not quickly enough. The club grazed her side, sending her tumbling from her horse. Nagar's heart stopped as he saw her hit the ground, her body limp.

"Irma!" he cried, dismounting and rushing to her side. The orcs closed in, but he didn't care. All that mattered was the woman lying before him, her breath coming in shallow gasps.

"Leave me," she whispered, her voice weak, her eyes half-lidded. "Save yourself."

Nagar shook his head, his hands trembling as he placed them over the wound. He closed his eyes, focusing on the healing spell Irma had once used on him. He could feel his life force draining, his energy sapping as he channeled it into her. The world spun around him, but he didn't stop. He couldn't stop.

"A life without you is no life at all," he murmured, his voice hoarse. "You were wrong, Irma. There's no one I'd rather be with than you."

Irma managed a faint smile, her hand reaching for his. "Fool," she whispered, her voice laced with affection.

But before Nagar could respond, the orcs were upon them. Strong hands grabbed him, pulling him away from Irma. He struggled, but he was weakened, his strength sapped by the spell. The orcs dragged him and Irma to the village center, where a crowd had gathered, their eyes gleaming with malicious intent.

The orcs began to argue over their fate, their voices a cacophony of growls and grunts.

"They'd make a fine wedding present for the chief," one orc suggested, a cruel grin spreading across his face. "After he consummates his marriage to the princess, he'll want entertainment. We can make these warriors fight to the death."

The others nodded in agreement; their eyes gleaming with anticipation. Nagar's heart sank as he realized their fate was sealed. They were to be pawns in the orcs' twisted game, their lives at the mercy of their captors.

Irma stirred beside him, her eyes flickering open. She looked at him, her expression a mix of fear and determination. "We'll find a way out of this," she whispered, her voice barely audible.

Nagar managed a weak smile, his hand brushing hers. "Together," he replied, his voice steady despite the fear gnawing at him.

The orcs hauled them away, their grip unyielding. Nagar glanced back at Irma, their eyes meeting for a fleeting moment. In that instant, he saw everything—her strength, her vulnerability, the depth of her love. And he knew, no matter what happened, he would never let her go.

They were taken to a crude cell, the bars thick and unyielding. The orcs left them there, the sound of their laughter echoing through the village. Nagar sat beside Irma, his arm around her, their bodies pressed together in a silent promise of solidarity.

"What now?" Irma asked, her voice quiet, her eyes searching his.

Nagar took a deep breath, his mind racing. "We wait," he said, his voice firm. "And we plan. We're not done yet, Irma. Not by a long shot."

She nodded, her hand tightening around his. The cell was dark, the air thick with the smell of damp earth and decay. But in that moment, with Irma by his side, Nagar felt a glimmer of hope. They were alive. They were together. And as long as they had each other, they had a chance.

Outside, the orcs continued their preparations for the chief's wedding, their voices a constant reminder of the danger that awaited them. But inside the cell, Nagar and Irma sat in silence, their hearts beating in unison, their bond stronger than ever.

The night fell, the sky a canvas of stars, the moon a silver crescent hanging low. Nagar leaned his head against the wall, his eyes closed, his mind racing. He thought of the princess, of the mission that had brought them here. He thought of the choices they had made, the paths they had taken. And he thought of Irma, of the woman who had become his everything.

He opened his eyes, meeting hers in the dim light. "We'll get out of this," he said, his voice a whisper. "I promise."

Irma smiled, her hand brushing his cheek. "I know," she replied, her voice soft, her eyes filled with a love that needed no words.

And in that moment, as the world outside teetered on the edge of chaos, Nagar and Irma found solace in each other, their love a beacon in the darkness, a promise of a future yet to come.

But as the night deepened, and the orcs' laughter grew louder, Nagar couldn't shake the feeling that their ordeal was far from over. The chief's wedding was tomorrow, and with it, their fate would be decided.

The tension was palpable, the air thick with anticipation. Nagar and Irma sat in silence, their minds racing, their hearts heavy. They knew what awaited them—a fight to the death, a spectacle for the orcs' amusement. But they also knew they had each other, and that was enough.

As the first light of dawn crept through the bars of their cell, Nagar turned to Irma, his hand gripping hers. "Ready?" he asked, his voice steady, his eyes determined.

Irma nodded, her expression resolute. "Always. Any ideas on how to get out of this? I don't feel like dying today."

"I could challenge the Orc chief."

"That's too dangerous! Orcs are stronger than most humans, and orc chiefs are the best fighters in the entire village."

"I know but it's the only way. Orcs live by a strict code of strength. Only the strongest can lead. If I kill their leader, I can become chief and demand the release of you and the princess."

"Yes, but at what cost?"

"I would rather die than you fight you." Nagar whispered. "I love you, Irma."

Irma's almond eyes opened wide at his admission.

Nagar smiled, "that's right I said it. I've known you for years Irma. You're by best friend, the person I count on most in this world. After having sex with you, something awakened inside me. I feel for you. I see you now in a different light. Not as a friend, but as a lover. I understand if you don't love me too, but..."

Irma's voice trembled as she whispered, "No, I love you. I love you so much," her words barely audible over the pounding of their hearts. Without hesitation, she lunged forward, tackling Nagar to the ground with a force that was both desperate and tender. Their bodies collided, and in that moment, the world around them seemed to fade away. Irma's lips found his, and their kiss ignited with a raw, unfiltered passion. It wasn't just a kiss—it was a declaration, a surrender, a plea for eternity in an instant.

Nagar's arms wrapped tightly around her, his grip firm yet trembling, as if afraid to let her go. Irma's fingers dug into his shoulders, her nails pressing into his skin as if to leave a mark, a reminder that this moment had happened. Their moans intertwined, a symphony of longing and fear, as the kiss deepened. Every emotion they had ever felt for each other poured into that embrace: joy, sorrow, hope, and the unspoken terror that this might be their final moment together.

The ground beneath them was hard and unforgiving, but they barely noticed. Their bodies pressed closer, as if trying to merge into one, to defy the uncertainty of the future. Nagar's breath quickened, his heart racing against Irma's chest, and she responded in kind, her lips moving feverishly against his. The air around them seemed to thicken, heavy with the weight of their shared vulnerability.

For a fleeting second, Irma pulled back just enough to meet his gaze, her eyes glistening with unshed tears. Nagar's expression mirrored hers—a mix of love and desperation. Without a word, they leaned in again, their lips locking once more, as if to seal a promise neither could voice. The world held its breath, and time stood still, if only for them.

When they finally parted, both were breathless, their chests rising and falling in sync. Irma rested her forehead against Nagar's, her hands still clutching him as if he were her anchor in a storm. Nagar closed his eyes, his fingers tracing the contours of her face, memorizing every detail. Neither spoke, for words could not capture what they had just shared. In that moment, they knew that whatever came next, they had given each other everything they had.

"If you do challenge the orc, promise me one thing." Irma grinned.

"What's that?"

"Don't die."

"I'd never dream of it." He grinned.

Chapter 5

The air in the orc village was thick with the scent of smoke and unwashed bodies, a pungent reminder of their captivity. Nagar stood tall in the center of the chief's hall, his breath steady despite the chaos swirling around him. The weight of Irma's kiss still lingered on his lips, her fierce promise echoing in his mind. **You better not die.** He clung to those words like a talisman, a fragile hope in the face of the impossible.

The hall was a cavernous space, its walls lined with the pelts of fallen beasts and the skulls of conquered enemies. Torches flickered, casting long shadows that danced across the dirt floor. The orcs gathered around him, their brutish forms a sea of muscle and scarred flesh. Their chief, a towering figure with a face like a jagged cliff, stood before him, his massive axe resting casually on his shoulder. The weapon gleamed with a dark, oily sheen, its edge notched from countless battles.

Nagar's voice cut through the murmurs of the crowd, sharp and clear. "I challenge your chief for his leadership," he declared, his words ringing with defiance. "In single combat. If I win, I become your chief, and you will let us leave with the princess."

The orcs erupted into laughter, a cacophony of grunts and jeers that filled the hall. One of them, a hulking brute with a missing ear, stepped forward, his lips curling into a sneer. "You? Challenge our chief, Oz? You'll only die, human. Just take the easy path to live and kill the elf."

Nagar's eyes narrowed towards Oz his gaze unwavering. "It is dishonorable to refuse a challenge. Do you fear me?"

The orcs exchanged glances, their mockery fading into something akin to respect. Oz himself let out a low, rumbling chuckle, his eyes glinting with amusement. "Very well, human. Let's see if you're as brave as you are foolish."

The hall fell silent as Oz tossed his axe aside, the weapon clattering to the ground with a resounding thud. He flexed his massive hands, cracking his knuckles with a sound like snapping bones. "I accept your challenge. I could use a bit of excitement before I fuck the princess."

Nagar's eyes darted towards Princess Vanessa who stood helplessly next to the chief. She was taller than Irma, with pale skin and blonde hair. Her clothes were muddy and torn. Despite being held prisoner she showed no fear.

The large orc flexed his muscles and said, "you can choose what ever weapon you want, but it won't matter, I will beat you with my bare hands. You are no match for my strength. Using my ax to kill you would be dishonorable so I will end your life with my fists."

"I choose my sword."

The chief nodded and looked at his guards. "Bring him his weapon."

The guards tossed Nagar his great sword and unbound his hands.

The orc chief laughed and held his fists up, "Know that—no one has ever bested me. You will die here, and your elf will join you."

Nagar's heart pounded in his chest, but his face remained impassive. He drew his sword, the steel singing as it slid from its sheath. The blade was a relic from long ago, its edge honed to a razor's keenness. Beside him, Irma stood chained to the wall, her eyes wide with fear and pride. She mouthed the words, *I love you*, and Nagar felt a surge of determination.

The chief lunged first, his speed belying his size. His fists were like hammers, each blow capable of shattering bone. Nagar dodged the first strike, his movements fluid and precise. He countered with a slash of his sword, but Oz caught the blade with one hand, his grip like iron. Nagar's arm trembled under the strain, but he refused to yield. With a single punch, Oz connected to Nagar's rib cage, and Nagar screamed in pain. He fell to his knees coughing blood. Oz kicked him, sending Nagar flying back.

"Nagar!" Irma screamed as Nagar rolled on the floor like a ragdoll. He could barely get up before Oz as in top of him again, kicking and punching him. Nagar swung his sword wildly connecting to Oz's thigh. Oz growled in pain, and Nagar retreated back to regain his footing. He stood with his sword at the ready. Oz grinned and then lunged at Nagar's as they traded blows once more.

The fight was brutal, a dance of steel and flesh. Oz's strength was overwhelming, each strike forcing Nagar to give ground. Blood-stained Nagar's armor as the chief's fist connected with his shoulder, sending him reeling. The pain was searing, but Nagar pushed it aside, focusing on his opponent.

Oz grinned, his teeth yellow and jagged. "You're strong, human. But not strong enough."

Nagar's breath came in ragged gasps, his vision blurring at the edges. He knew he couldn't last much longer. The chief raised his fist for the killing blow, his eyes gleaming with triumph.

In that moment, Nagar saw his opening. With a desperate lunge, he drove his sword into the chief's thigh, the blade sinking deep into the muscle. The chief roared in pain, dropping to one knee. Nagar seized the moment, plunging his sword into the orc's chest.

The hall fell silent as Oz toppled forward, his massive form hitting the ground with a thud. Nagar stood panting, his chest heaving, his sword still buried in the orc's chest. For a moment, he thought it was over.

Then, one by one, the orcs around him dropped to their knees, bowing their heads. Nagar's lips curled into a weary smile as he realized he'd succeeded. He was their chief now.

But the victory was bittersweet. Irma remained chained to the wall, her eyes searching his face. Princess Vanessa, a delicate figure with a crown of braids, watched from the shadows, her expression unreadable. Nagar sheathed his sword, his movements slow and deliberate. He walked to Irma, his boots echoing on the dirt floor. With all the strength he had, he unbound her shackles and then fell forward into her arms.

As Irma held him, he whispered, "We're free."

Irma's lips trembled as she nodded, "You fought bravely. I love you..." she placed her hands on his chest and they glowed as she healed him. Once he was fully healed, she kissed him. "You did it."

Nagar's smile brightened as he no longer felt any pain. With renewed strength he turned to face the orcs. His eyes narrowed staring at each orc before him. They knelt before him, their faces a mix of awe and fear. He was their leader now, but the weight of that responsibility settled heavily on his shoulders. The princess stood apart from the crowd, her wide-eyed gaze fixed on Nagar.

"What happens now?" Irma asked, her voice barely above a whisper as she stood next to him.

Nagar's eyes met hers, his expression grim. "Now, we figure out how to lead a tribe of orcs and rescue a princess. And somehow, we find a way to be together."

The orcs began to stir, their murmurs growing louder. Nagar raised a hand, silencing them. "I am your chief now," he declared, his voice steady. "But I do not seek to rule through fear. I seek to lead through strength and honor. Now we will find a new path, one that does not require bloodshed."

The orcs exchanged glances; their faces uncertain. Nagar knew he had to tread carefully. These were not the mindless brutes of legend; they were a people with their own customs and beliefs. He was a human, and they've never been led by a creature not themselves. He had to earn their trust, not just their obedience.

Princess Vanessa stepped forward, her voice soft but commanding. "You have proven yourself, Chief Nagar. But what of me? Am I'm free?"

Nagar's gaze flickered to Irma, then back to the princess. "Yes, your Highness. We will find a way to ensure your safety, back home if that is what you wish."

The princess studied him for a moment, her expression unreadable. "Yes, please take me home."

Irma's hand found Nagar's, her grip tight and reassuring. The orcs began to rise, their faces a mix of curiosity and wariness. Nagar knew the road ahead would be fraught with challenges. He was now a leader of a tribe of orcs, still deliver the Princess to her father, and navigate his own complicated feelings for Irma—it was a daunting task.

But as he stood there, surrounded by the uncertain faces of his new tribe, Nagar felt a spark of hope. They were not just orcs; they were people, capable of change and growth. And perhaps, just perhaps, they could forge a new future together.

"I will take Princess Vanessa back to her castle."

"And what of us?" An orc asked.

"I'll ask two orcs help guide us back. The rest of you, when I return, we will talk more about our future together."

They all bowed and pounded their chests in agreement.

Later that day, the sun was setting as Nagar left the village, with Princess Vanessa, Irma and two new orc hunters named Thok and Grish. Nagar didn't know much about the two large creatures, but they were the only two who volunteered to assist him on his journey back, which was a step in building trust between him and the orcs.

As they left the gates of the village, the horizon was painted in hues of orange and purple, a breathtaking sight that seemed to promise new beginnings. Nagar took a deep breath, the cool evening air filling his lungs.

"Are you ready?" Irma asked, her voice laced with wonder as she stood next to him.

"Always," Nagar smiled, his gaze fixed on the horizon. "I'm ready for anything as long as we're together."

And with that, they walked into the unknown, their footsteps echoing on the ancient path. The future was uncertain, but for the first time in a long while, Nagar felt a sense of peace. They had survived the impossible, and now, anything seemed possible.

Chapter 6

The sun dipped below the horizon, casting an amber glow over the forest as Nagar and his companions made camp for the night. The air was thick with the scent of pine and damp earth, a soothing contrast to the blood and sweat of the previous days. Nagar, now the chief of the Wontrui orcs, felt the weight of his new responsibilities settle on his shoulders. Yet, as he gazed at Irma, her jet-black hair cascading over her shoulders, her almond-shaped eyes gleaming with quiet strength, he found solace in her presence. She was his anchor, his reason to keep moving forward.

The two orcs, Grish and Thok, set up the camp with efficient, practiced movements. They had been loyal to Oz, but Nagar's victory in combat had earned their respect, and they now followed him without question. Princess Vanessa, still reeling from her ordeal, sat by the fire, her regal demeanor tempered by exhaustion. Nagar assigned Grish and Thok to keep watch over her, ensuring her safety as he excused himself to clean up at the nearby lake.

The lake was a short walk from the camp, its surface smooth as glass, reflecting the fading light of the sky. Nagar stripped off his clothes, leaving them in a heap on the shore, and waded into the cool water. The chill sent a shiver through him, but it was refreshing after the heat of battle and the tension of leadership. He dunked his head, letting the water wash away the grime and sweat, and closed his eyes, savoring the moment of peace.

When he opened them again, he saw Irma standing on the shore, her silhouette framed by the twilight. Her clothes were still on, but her gaze was fixed on him, a mischievous smile playing on her lips. "What are you doing?" he called out, his voice echoing across the still water.

"Joining you," she replied, her voice soft but firm. Without hesitation, she began to undress, her movements deliberate and unhurried. Nagar watched, his breath catching in his throat as her clothes fell to the ground, revealing her petite, beige curves. Her skin glowed in the dim light, her small, perky tits rising and falling with her breath. Her deep almond-shaped eyes met his, and he felt a surge of desire so intense it left him lightheaded.

Irma waded into the water; her steps graceful despite the uneven ground. The cool liquid lapped at her thighs, then her waist, as she drew closer to him. Nagar reached out, pulling her into his arms. Their lips met in a hungry kiss, their tongues tangling as they clung to each other. His hands roamed her body, tracing the curves of her hips, the slope of her breasts, the delicate line of her spine. She pressed against him, her softness a stark contrast to his rugged build, and he groaned into her mouth, his cock hardening at the contact.

"I've wanted you since the moment I saw you," he murmured against her lips, his voice rough with need. "Every second we've been apart has been torture."

Irma smiled, her fingers threading through his wet hair. "Then take me," she whispered. "Here. Now. I'm yours, Nagar."

He didn't need to be told twice. With a growl, he lifted her, her legs wrapping around his waist as he pressed her against the nearest rock, the cool surface a stark contrast to the heat of their bodies. Their kisses grew more frantic, their breaths coming in short, ragged gasps. Nagar's hands moved between them, his fingers brushing against her core, already wet and eager for him.

"Fuck, you're ready for me," he groaned, his voice thick with desire. "So, fucking wet. I can't wait any longer."

He positioned himself at her entrance, his throbbing cock aching to be inside her. With a slow, deliberate thrust, he entered her, their bodies merging as one. Irma gasped, her head falling back as he filled her completely. The water lapped around them, the sounds of the forest a distant backdrop to their passionate union.

"Ride me," he commanded, his voice hoarse. "Show me how much you want me."

Irma obeyed, her hips moving in a rhythm that matched his own. She moaned loudly, her hands gripping his shoulders as she rode him with abandon. Nagar watched her, his eyes drinking in the sight of her petite frame moving above him, her tits bouncing with each thrust. He reached up, cupping them in his hands, his thumbs brushing over her tight dark nipples. She shivered, her movements becoming more urgent as he teased her, his touch sending sparks of pleasure through her body.

"Harder," she panted, her voice barely audible over the sound of the water. "Fuck me harder, Nagar. I need you."

He didn't hold back. With a growl, he flipped her, pressing her against the rock as he took control. His thrusts became more forceful, his cock pounding into her with a rhythm that left them both breathless. The water splashed around them, mixing with their sweat and the slickness of their passion. Irma's moans grew louder, her body trembling as she neared the edge.

"Cum for me," he demanded, his voice a raw whisper. "Let me feel you fall apart around my cock."

Her orgasm hit her like a wave, her body convulsing as she cried out his name. Nagar felt her pussy tighten around him, milking his cock as she rode out her release. It was too much for him to bear. With a final, powerful thrust, he followed her over the edge, his cum shooting deep inside her as he roared her name.

They clung to each other, their hearts pounding in unison as they caught their breath. Nagar held her tightly, his lips pressing against her sweat-dampened hair. "I love you," he whispered, his voice thick with emotion. "I'll never let you go."

Irma smiled, her fingers tangling in his hair. "I love you too," she replied, her voice soft but steady. "We'll face whatever comes next together."

For a moment, they stayed like that, their bodies still joined, the world around them fading into insignificance. But the night was far from over, and the forest held secrets yet to be uncovered. As they waded back to shore, hand in hand, Nagar couldn't shake the feeling that their peace was fleeting. The journey ahead would be fraught with challenges, but with Irma by his side, he knew they could weather any storm.

Back at the camp, the fire crackled, casting flickering shadows across the clearing. Grish and Thok sat by the flames, their eyes alert as they kept watch over Princess Vanessa. She lay wrapped in a blanket, her breathing steady, but Nagar noticed the tension in her shoulders, the way her hands clenched and unclenched in her lap. She was far from safe, and the weight of her rescue rested heavily on his shoulders.

Irma noticed his gaze and followed it to the princess. "She's been through a lot," she said softly, her hand squeezing his. "But she's strong. She'll make it through this."

Nagar nodded, though his mind was already racing with plans. The castle was still days away, and the forest was full of dangers. The Wontrui orcs were loyal, but there were other tribes, other threats lurking in the shadows. And then there was the matter of his new role as chief—a role he was still learning to navigate.

"We'll rest here tonight," he said, his voice firm. "But come morning, we move quickly. The sooner we get her home, the better."

Irma nodded, her expression resolute. "We'll make it," she said, her voice a promise. "Together."

As they settled by the fire, Nagar couldn't help but steal glances at Irma, her beauty illuminated by the dancing flames. She caught his eye and smiled, her hand reaching out to lace their fingers together. The warmth of her touch was a balm to his soul, a reminder of what they were fighting for.

But as the night deepened, and the forest grew quiet, Nagar found himself unable to sleep. He lay beside Irma, her steady breathing a soothing rhythm, but his mind was a whirlwind of thoughts. The challenge of leading the Wontrui, the responsibility of protecting Princess Vanessa, the uncertainty of their future—it all weighed on him. And yet, amidst the chaos, there was Irma, her love a beacon in the darkness.

He turned to her, his hand brushing a stray lock of hair from her face. She stirred, her eyes fluttering open, and he saw the question in her gaze. "What's wrong?" she murmured, her voice thick with sleep.

"Nothing," he lied, his thumb tracing the curve of her cheek. "I was just thinking about us. About everything we've been through."

Irma smiled, her hand covering his. "We've faced worse," she said softly. "And we'll face whatever comes next together. That's all that matters."

Nagar leaned in, his lips brushing hers in a tender kiss. "You're right," he whispered. "Together."

But as he closed his eyes, the forest seemed to close in around them, the shadows deepening, the silence heavy with unspoken fears. The night was far from over, and the journey ahead would test them in ways they couldn't yet imagine. Yet, in that moment, with Irma by his side, Nagar felt a glimmer of hope. Whatever lay ahead, they would face it together, their love a shield against the darkness.

The fire crackled, casting flickering shadows across the camp, and the forest held its breath, waiting to see what the dawn would bring. For now, they rested, their hearts beating as one, their story far from over.

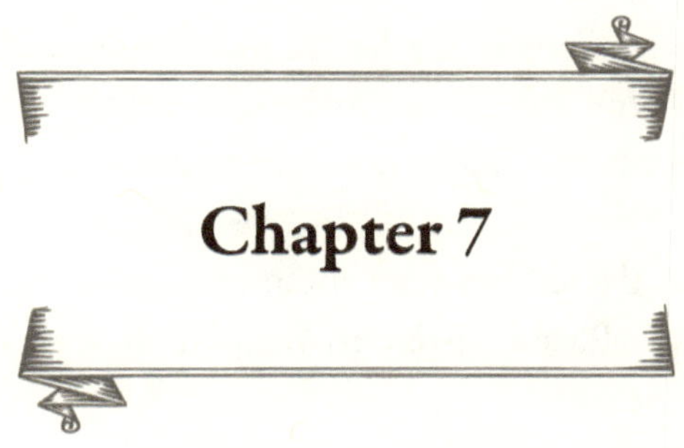

Chapter 7

The forest, bathed in the soft glow of twilight, had seemed a sanctuary mere hours ago. Now, it was a battleground. The mercenaries, their faces twisted with determination and greed, emerged from the shadows like specters, their armor glinting faintly in the moonlight. Their leader, a grizzled man with a scar running down his cheek, stepped forward, his voice harsh and commanding. "Hand over the princess, and we'll spare the rest of you."

Princess Vanessa, her golden hair tousled and her eyes wide with fear, stepped forward, her hands raised in a gesture of peace. "Please, I'm safe. These orcs—Grish and Thok—they didn't kidnap me. It's complicated, but they're not like the others. Please, don't hurt them." Her voice trembled, but there was a steel beneath it, a determination to protect those who had become her unlikely allies.

The mercenaries exchanged glances, their skepticism evident. "Orcs are orcs," the leader growled, his hand resting on the hilt of his sword. "And they've got you. We're not leaving without you."

Nagar, his broad shoulders tense and his eyes narrowed, stepped beside Vanessa. Irma, her bow already drawn, stood at his side, her expression a mix of defiance and concern. Grish and Thok, their massive forms looming in the dim light, exchanged a glance before shifting their stances, ready to defend their companions.

"She's right," Nagar said, his deep voice cutting through the tension. "These orcs are different. They've sworn loyalty to me, and they've done nothing wrong."

The mercenaries laughed, a harsh, mocking sound. "Orcs loyal to a human chief? You expect us to believe that?" The leader's hand tightened on his sword. "We're not here to debate. Step aside, or we'll cut through you."

Vanessa's eyes darted between the mercenaries and her protectors, her mind racing. "Please, listen to me. Grish and Thok saved me. They're not the enemy."

But the mercenaries were beyond reason, their minds clouded by the promise of gold and glory. With a roar, the leader lunged forward, his sword slicing through the air. The battle began.

Grish and Thok moved as one, their brutish strength and battle-hardened instincts turning the tide. Grish, his massive frame a wall of muscle, intercepted the leader's attack, his own blade clashing against the mercenary's with a deafening ring. Thok, his movements deceptively swift for his size, charged another mercenary, his warhammer crashing into the man's shield with enough force to send him sprawling.

Nagar and Irma joined the fray, their combat skills honed by years of survival and battle. Nagar's sword flashed in the moonlight, each strike precise and deadly. Irma's arrows flew true, finding their marks with unerring accuracy. The camp erupted into chaos, the sounds of steel on steel and grunts of exertion filling the air.

Despite their large numbers, the mercenaries found themselves on the defensive. Grish and Thok fought with a ferocity born of loyalty and a desire to prove themselves. They moved in tandem, their attacks coordinated and relentless. Nagar's leadership was evident as he directed the defense, his commands clear and decisive. Irma's skill with the bow added an unpredictable element, with her defensive shots covering her allies blindsides and her offensive shots disrupting the mercenaries' formations.

The battle raged on, the forest becoming a stage for a brutal dance of life and death. The mercenaries, though skilled, were no match for the unity and determination of Nagar's group. One by one, they fell, their cries of pain and defeat echoing through the trees.

As the last mercenary lay defeated, the group stood amidst the wreckage of the camp, their breaths coming in ragged gasps. Grish and Thok, their armor dented and their faces smeared with dirt and blood, exchanged a nod, a silent acknowledgment of their shared victory.

Nagar sheathed his sword, his eyes scanning the battlefield. "We're not safe here," he said, his voice grim. "We need to move, now."

Vanessa, her face pale but her eyes determined, nodded. "Wherever we go, we go together. Grish and Thok have proven themselves. They're part of this now."

Irma, her bow slung over her shoulder, placed a hand on Nagar's arm. "We'll find a way. Together."

The group gathered their belongings, the tension of the battle still lingering in the air. As they prepared to leave, Nagar turned to Grish and Thok, his expression softening. "You've earned my trust. And for that, I'm grateful."

Grish grunted, a rare smile tugging at the corners of his mouth. "We fight for you, Chief. And for her." He gestured to Vanessa.

Thok nodded, his eyes serious. "We will protect her. With our lives, if necessary."

Nagar clapped them both on the shoulder, a gesture of camaraderie and respect. "Then let's move. The king's men won't be far behind, and we've got a princess to return."

As they disappeared into the forest, the moon casting long shadows in their wake, the night seemed to hold its breath. The battle was over, but the journey was far from finished. The bonds forged in the heat of combat would be tested again, and the road ahead was fraught with uncertainty. Yet, as they walked, their steps were steady, their resolve unshakable. Together, they would face whatever came next, their fates intertwined in a tapestry of loyalty, love, and adventure.

The forest whispered secrets in the wind, ancient tales of heroes and villains, of magic and mystery. And in that moment, as Nagar, Irma, Vanessa, Grish, and Thok ventured into the unknown, they became part of that story, their legend unfolding with each step they took. The world was vast, and their journey had only just begun.

Chapter 8

The grand gates of the Green Kingdom loomed before them, their iron bars twisted into the shape of ancient vines, a testament to the kingdom's namesake. The air was thick with the scent of blooming flowers, a stark contrast to the tension that gripped Nagar, Irma, Grish, and Thok as they approached the entrance. Princess Vanessa rode beside Nagar, her face pale but determined, her golden hair cascading over the shoulders of her travel-worn cloak. Behind them, the forest whispered secrets of their harrowing journey, but ahead lay the unknown—a kingdom that had once been a beacon of hope, now a potential battleground.

The guards at the gate lowered their spears as Vanessa raised a hand, her voice carrying the authority of royalty. "Open the gates. I have returned."

The portcullis creaked upward, its chains groaning under the weight of centuries. The group rode through, their horses' hooves clattering on the cobblestones. The streets of the Green Kingdom were alive with color—banners of emerald and gold fluttered in the breeze, and merchants called out their wares from stalls overflowing with fruits, spices, and handcrafted goods. Yet, the usual bustle seemed muted, as if the kingdom held its breath, awaiting the return of its princess.

From the city square, the castle came into view, its white stone gleaming in the afternoon sun. Its towers pierced the sky, adorned with intricate carvings of leaves and vines. Guards lined the path to the throne room, their armor polished to a mirror shine, their faces stern. Nagar felt Irma's hand brush his, a silent gesture of solidarity. Grish and Thok exchanged a glance, their massive forms tense, ready for any threat.

King Hector sat upon his throne, his crown resting heavily on his brow. His eyes, a deep emerald like his daughter's, narrowed focusing on the orcs and elf in his presence, but as Vanessa approached his eyes soften their tone. For a moment, the room was silent, the only sound the faint rustle of the tapestry depicting the kingdom's founding. Then, Hector rose, his movements stiff, his voice trembling with emotion.

"Vanessa," he choked out, his arms opening as if to embrace her.

"Daddy..." she ran and hugged her father. After their embrace he turned faced Nagar.

"Sell sword, what's your name?"

"Nagar, your majesty."

"Nagar...do you have any royal blood?"

"No, your majesty."

"Ah, well then, your luck has changed. You will be rewarded with riches and of course my daughter's hand in marriage..."

Nagar eyes darted towards Irma who frowned at him.

Nagar cleared his throat and replied, "thank you, King Hector, but I only want the gold. Please allow the princess to marry whom she wants."

Irma smiled at Nagar, and he winked back at her.

"What?" The king snapped. "You disagree with a king's decree? You know how many men will kill and die for your position? To be honored by the king and be granted royalty? Tell me what other woman has your gaze?"

"Irma, my king. I love her." Nagar replied, boldly. He took the elf's hand and stood up straight on the presence of the king.

King Hector's cheeks went red. "Her! That disgusting elf? You'd want to taint your human lineage with that!"

"Yes, she means more to me than you know..."

King Hector shook his head, "first you defy me, refusing the hand of my daughter only to take the hand of a half breed like that elf, then you disgrace my presence with these disgusting creatures!" He glared at Irma, Grish and Thok.

Vanessa stepped forward; her voice steady. "Father, Irma, Grish and Thok saved my life. Without them, I would not be standing here before you."

Hector's eyes flashed with anger. "Orcs and Elves are not to be trusted. They are wild beasts and half breeds, nothing more." He turned to his guards. "Seize them. Take them to the dungeons. We will deal with them later."

Nagar stepped forward, his hand resting on the hilt of his sword. "Your Majesty, they had no part in the princess's capture. They are under my protection."

The king's laughter was cold. "Protection? You, a sell-sword, presume to protect my daughter and my kingdom? You will be placed in the dungeon never to see the light of day again. The elf will be banished back to her lands. And these... orcs? They are an abomination. They will be executed, and their tribes will be eradicated."

Irma's voice was sharp, her elven accent cutting through the tension. "Your Majesty, the Wontrui tribe has done nothing to warrant such an attack. Nagar is their chief now. He has sworn to keep the peace."

Hector's face turned purple with rage. "You dare speak to me as if yourself is human!" This is treason!" He pointed a trembling finger at Nagar. "Guards! Arrest them all!"

Vanessa stepped between her father and the group; her hands raised. "Father, please! They are not your enemies. They are my friends. They risked their lives for me."

"Friends?" Hector's voice was a whisper, dangerous in its calm. "You would side with them over your own family? Over your kingdom?"

The room erupted into chaos. Guards drew their swords, their eyes fixed on Nagar, Irma, Grish, and Thok. Nagar's hand closed around the hilt of his blade, his mind racing. He had not come here to fight, but it seemed fight was all the king would offer.

"We don't want a battle," Nagar said, his voice steady despite the storm within him. "But we will not be taken without a fight."

Irma's bow was already in her hands, an arrow nocked and aimed at the nearest guard. Grish and Thok stood back-to-back, their weapons gleaming in the light of the throne room's chandeliers. The air was electric, charged with the promise of violence.

"Kill them!" Hector roared, his voice echoing through the hall.

The first guard lunged at Nagar, his sword slashing downward. Nagar sidestepped, his own blade meeting the guards in a clash of steel. Irma's arrow flew true, striking the guard in the shoulder, sending him reeling. Grish roared, his axe cleaving through the air, taking down two guards in a single swing. Thok's massive frame was a whirlwind of fury, his war hammer a blur as he carved a path through the ranks.

Vanessa cried out, her voice lost in the chaos. Nagar's heart ached as he fought, knowing that every strike brought him further from the peace he had hoped to achieve. Irma fought with precision, her movements graceful yet deadly, her elven magic adding an otherworldly edge to her attacks.

The battle was brief but brutal. Bodies lay strewn across the throne room, the once-pristine floor now stained with blood. Nagar's breath came in ragged gasps as he faced the last of the guards, his arms trembling with exhaustion. Irma stood beside him, her bow lowered, her face pale. Grish and Thok stood back-to-back, their weapons dripping with blood, their chests heaving.

King Hector stood frozen, his eyes wide with shock and rage. "Traitors!" he spat, his voice shaking. "You will never escape. The entire kingdom will hunt you down. You will be remembered as criminals, as enemies of the Green Kingdom."

Nagar sheathed his sword, his voice heavy with regret. "We did not come here to be enemies, Your Majesty. But if that is what you choose, so be it."

Vanessa stepped forward, her eyes filled with tears. "Father, please. This is not the way. They are not your enemies."

Hector's gaze was cold as he turned to his daughter. "You are no longer my daughter if you stand with them. Get out of my way or face the consequences."

Vanessa's shoulders sagged, but her voice was firm. "I will not abandon them. They are my friends, and they are innocent."

While the two royals glared at each other, Nagar used this opportunity to turn and run from the throne room, Irma, Grish, and Thok following closely behind. Vanessa hesitated for a moment, and then rushed after them, her footsteps echoing in the empty hall.

The streets of the Green Kingdom were silent as they passed, the citizens watching from behind closed doors and shuttered windows. The group gather their horses and rode in silence, the weight of their actions pressing down on them. Nagar's mind was a whirlwind of thoughts—regret, anger, and a deep sense of betrayal. He had hoped to bring peace, to bridge the gap between humans and orcs, but instead, he had become an outlaw, a fugitive in the eyes of the kingdom.

As they reached the forest's edge, Nagar turned to the group, his voice grim. "We need to get back to the Wontrui village. It's the only place we'll be safe."

Irma nodded, her face drawn. "We'll need to move quickly. The king's men will be after us soon."

Grish grunted, his massive hands tightening on the reins of his horse. "We will fight. We will not let them destroy our home."

Thok's voice was low, his eyes dark with determination. "We stand with you, Nagar. To the end."

Vanessa's voice was soft but resolute. "I'm with you as well. I will not let my father's hatred destroy the lives of those who saved me."

Nagar's heart swelled with gratitude, but his mind was already racing ahead, planning their next move. The journey back to the Wontrui village would be perilous, and the kingdom's forces would be hot on their heels. They would need to move swiftly, to use the forest's cover to their advantage.

As they rode deeper into the forest, the trees seemed to close in around them, their branches intertwining like protective arms. The air was cool, the scent of pine and earth filling their lungs. Nagar felt a sense of calm wash over him, a reminder that they were not alone. The forest itself seemed to be on their side, a silent ally in their quest for survival.

Chapter 9

The sun dipped below the jagged horizon, casting the forest in hues of amber and violet as the group pressed onward, their footsteps muffled by the thick carpet of fallen leaves. The air was heavy with the scent of pine and the distant tang of smoke, a reminder of the Green Kingdom they had left behind in flames. Irma, Nagar, Grish, Thok, and Princess Vanessa moved with purpose, their eyes scanning the shadows for any sign of pursuit. The soldiers of King Hector had proven relentless, their ambushes growing more frequent and more desperate with each passing league.

Irma, her bow slung across her back, walked with a quiet intensity. Her elven senses were on high alert, her ears twitching at every rustle of foliage. Nagar, his sword sheathed but his hand never far from the hilt, kept a steady pace beside her. The bond between them, forged in blood and fire, was unspoken but palpable. Grish, the younger orc, trudged behind them, his eyes darting nervously between the trees. Thok, his massive frame a bulwark of muscle and scarred skin, brought up the rear, his gaze fixed on Vanessa.

The princess herself walked with a newfound resolve, her once-delicate hands now calloused from gripping a sword. She had shed the trappings of royalty, trading her silken gowns for practical leathers, but the weight of her crown still lingered in her eyes. She glanced back at Thok, her expression a mix of gratitude and unease. The orc's presence was a constant reminder of the peril they faced, but also of the protection he offered.

The forest seemed to close in around them, the trees towering like silent sentinels. The path ahead twisted and turned, leading them deeper into the heart of the woods. Suddenly, a sharp whistle pierced the air, followed by the thunder of hooves. Vanessa's eyes widened as a group of soldiers emerged from the underbrush, their armor glinting in the fading light.

"Ambush!" Nagar roared, drawing his sword in a single fluid motion. Irma nocked an arrow, her movements precise and deadly. Grish let out a guttural growl, his hands clenching into fists as he prepared to fight. Thok stepped forward, his massive form blocking Vanessa from harm.

"Stay behind me," he rumbled, his voice a low growl.

The soldiers charged, their swords raised and their battle cries echoing through the forest. Nagar met the first attacker head-on, his blade flashing in the dim light. Irma's arrow flew true, finding its mark in the throat of a soldier who had aimed for Vanessa. Grish lunged forward, his fists pounding into the chest of an attacker, sending the man sprawling.

Thok stood like a mountain, his massive arms deflecting blows with ease. He swung his war hammer in a wide arc, the weapon cracking against armor and bone alike. Vanessa, her heart pounding, drew her own sword, her movements tentative but determined. As a child she'd had some training with a blade, but never thought she'd use it to survive. Back then it was only for play, but as soon as she turned ten, she turned in her wooden sword for a crown becoming a princess she was today. Now, she used those skills she learned as a child to survive. She used them to fight against the men who once swore an oath to her. For that brief moment, she didn't think about her father or her kingdom, she only thought about drawing her next breath.

She parried a strike, her blade trembling in her grip, the shocking vibrations made her lower her guard, but before the soldier could land the killing blow, Thok was there in an instant, his weapon smashing the soldier aside.

"Focus on your footing and only pick off whom I've weakened," he grunted, his eyes never leaving the fray. "Let me handle the rest."

Vanessa nodded as she moved into a defensive position waiting to stab any man on the ground recovering from Thok's mighty blows from his hammer.

The battle was brutal and brief, the soldiers falling one by one to the group's coordinated assault. As the last man collapsed to the ground, the forest fell silent once more, the only sound the heavy breathing of the survivors. Vanessa leaned against a tree, her sword slipping from her grasp as she stared at the carnage around her.

"You fought well," Thok replied, slinging his war hammer around his back.

"I've never killed anyone before," Vanessa admitted, her hands shaking as they were covered in blood.

"It gets easier." Thok replied. "It was either them or you."

"I... I can't believe they'd do this," she whispered, her voice shaking. "My father's men... trying to kill me."

Thok turned to her, his expression grim but gentle. "They follow orders, Princess. But they won't harm you while I'm here."

Vanessa managed a small smile, her eyes lingering on the scars that marked his battle-hardened body. "Thank you," she said softly. "For everything."

Thok nodded, his gaze steady. "It's what I'm here for."

As night fell, the group pressed on, the forest growing darker and more foreboding. They found a clearing surrounded by tall trees, their branches intertwining to form a natural canopy. Irma and Nagar set about gathering firewood, their movements efficient and practiced. Grish helped Vanessa gather kindling, his awkward attempts at conversation met with her tentative smiles.

Thok stood watch, his eyes scanning the treeline for any sign of danger. The fire crackled to life, its warmth a welcome relief against the chill of the night. Vanessa sat cross-legged by the flames, her hands clasped tightly in her lap. She stared into the dancing flames, her thoughts a whirlwind of confusion and fear.

After a moment, she rose and approached Thok, her steps hesitant. "Can I... can I talk to you?" she asked, her voice barely above a whisper.

Thok turned to her, his expression softening. "Of course."

She sat down beside him, her shoulders hunched as if bearing the weight of the world. "I was wrong about orcs," she admitted, her voice trembling. "I thought... I thought you were all monsters. But you've shown me otherwise."

Thok's gaze dropped to the ground, his massive hands clasped between his knees. "Not all of us followed Oz willingly," he said, his tone reflective. "His ambitions were his own, not ours. Capturing you... that was a line crossed, and for that, I'm sorry."

Vanessa's smile softened, and she placed a hand on his arm. "I forgive you," she said, her words carrying a weight of understanding and acceptance.

Thok looked up, his eyes meeting hers. In that moment, the barriers between them seemed to crumble, replaced by a bond forged in shared struggle and mutual respect. The fire crackled between them, its warmth a mirror to the growing connection.

As the night deepened, the group settled into an uneasy sleep, their rest punctuated by the occasional crackle of the fire and the distant calls of nocturnal creatures. Irma lay beside Nagar, her hand entwined with his, their bond a source of strength in the face of uncertainty. Grish slept fitfully, his dreams haunted by the violence of the day. Vanessa curled up near Thok, her sleep troubled but comforted by his presence.

Thok himself remained awake, his eyes fixed on the stars that peeked through the canopy above. He thought of Oz, of the path that had led him here, and of the choices that had shaped his life. He thought of Vanessa, of the trust she had placed in him, and of the promise he had made to protect her.

The forest was alive with magic, its ancient trees whispering secrets to those who listened. The air was thick with the scent of pine and earth, a reminder of the world beyond their struggles. In the distance, a wolf howled, its call a haunting melody that echoed through the night.

As the first light of dawn crept over the horizon, Thok rose, his movements silent as he resumed his vigil. The others stirred, their faces etched with fatigue but their spirits resolute. They shared a meager breakfast of dried meat and bread, their conversation muted but their determination unwavering.

"We need to keep moving," Nagar said, his voice steady. "The soldiers won't stop until they've found us."

Irma nodded, her eyes scanning the treeline. "We'll need to find a safer route. The forest is vast, but it's also full of dangers."

Grish stood, his hands clenching into fists. "We'll face whatever comes," he said, his voice firm. "Together."

Vanessa rose, her sword at her side. She looked at Thok, her expression grateful. "Thank you," she said again, her words a quiet acknowledgment of his unwavering protection.

Thok nodded, his gaze steady. "Let's go."

The group set off once more, their footsteps echoing through the forest as they ventured deeper into the unknown. The trees loomed above them, their branches swaying gently in the breeze. The air was thick with the scent of adventure, of danger, and of the promise of new beginnings.

As they walked, Vanessa fell into step beside Thok, her presence a silent comfort. She glanced up at him, her eyes meeting his. In that moment, words were unnecessary. Their bond, forged in the crucible of battle and tempered by mutual respect, spoke volumes.

The forest stretched before them, its secrets waiting to be uncovered. The path ahead was uncertain, but together, they would face whatever lay in store. The journey was far from over, and the challenges they would face were many. But for now, they walked on, their hearts united and their spirits unyielding.

Chapter 10

The sun dipped below the horizon as the weary group emerged from the forest's edge, the ancient trees giving way to the sprawling village of the Wontrui. Smoke curled from the thatched roofs of the longhouses, mingling with the fading light, and the air carried the scent of woodsmoke and earth. Nagar, his human features standing in stark contrast to the green-skinned orcs around him, felt the weight of his newfound leadership settle heavier on his shoulders. He knew being chief would be difficult especially since he was human. However he made a promise to himself to take the honor seriously. He knew when he killed Oz, the title he earned wasn't just for his freedom.

As they walked through the open plain towards the gate, Nagar marveled at the sight before him. The village was a testament to the orcs' resilience—a place of rugged beauty and unyielding strength. Yet, beneath the surface calm, Nagar sensed a tension that prickled like the first chill of winter.

Irma, her elven grace belying the weariness in her eyes, walked beside him, her hand brushing his in a silent gesture of solidarity. Behind them, Grish and Thok moved with the quiet confidence of warriors accustomed to danger, while Princess Vanessa trailed, her gaze alternating between curiosity and unease. The village square was alive with activity, orcs going about their evening routines, but their glances toward Nagar and his companions were laced with suspicion and something darker—resentment.

"Something's wrong," Irma murmured, her voice low enough to carry only to Nagar. "They're not acting like we're their chief's family."

Nagar nodded, his jaw tightening. He had known this day would come, but he had hoped for more time to solidify his position. The Wontrui had accepted him as their leader after his victory over Chief Oz, but his human blood was a thorn in the side of tradition. He scanned the crowd, his eyes narrowing as he spotted a group of orcs huddled near the edge of the square, their voices low but their hostility palpable. Among them stood a towering figure, his muscular frame adorned with scars and a headdress of boar tusks—Kargoth, leader of the Bloodclaw clan, the most vocal of Nagar's detractors.

"We need to address this before it escalates," Nagar said, his voice steady despite the turmoil within him. "Come."

He led the group toward the central longhouse, the heart of the village, where the elders and clan leaders gathered. The air grew thicker with each step, the weight of unspoken words pressing down on them. Inside, the longhouse was dimly lit by flickering torches, their flames casting long shadows on the walls adorned with tapestries of past battles and hunts. The elders sat in a semicircle, their faces etched with age and wisdom, but their eyes held a wariness that Nagar had not seen before.

Kargoth stood at the forefront, his arms crossed, his gaze locked on Nagar with a mixture of defiance and disdain. "You dare call yourself chief," he growled, his voice rumbling like distant thunder. "A human, leading orcs. It is an insult to our ancestors."

Nagar stepped forward, his posture unwavering. "I earned this title in combat, as is the way of the orcs. I have bled for this clan, and I will continue to protect it."

"With human blood?" Kargoth scoffed. "You are an outsider, Nagar. You do not understand our ways, our traditions. The Wontrui deserve a leader who is one of us. A leader who is an orc!"

The group fell silent, the tension thick enough to cut with a blade. Nagar could feel the eyes of the elders on him, judging, questioning. He knew he had to tread carefully. A wrong word, a misstep, and the fragile alliance he had built could shatter.

"Our traditions are important," Nagar acknowledged, his tone measured. "But they are not the only thing that matters. The world is changing, Kargoth. Humans will encroach on orc lands, their greed knowing no bounds. They do not care about our traditions. They care only for conquest."

Kargoth's lips curled in a sneer. "And you think you can protect us? A human who has spent his life among them? You are a traitor to your own kind, and now you seek to lead us?"

Nagar's gaze hardened. "I am no traitor. I chose this path because I believe in it. Because I believe in the strength and honor of the Wontrui. But if we continue to fight among ourselves, we will fall. United, we stand a chance against the true threat."

Before Kargoth could respond, a commotion erupted outside the longhouse. Shouts and the clatter of weapons echoed through the village, breaking the tense silence. Nagar's heart sank as he recognized the cries—human voices, laced with aggression and fear.

"They've found us," Irma whispered, her hand instinctively reaching for the dagger at her belt.

Nagar turned to Kargoth, his eyes pleading. "Do you hear that? Those are the humans. They do not distinguish between us. To them, we are all enemies. Will you let them divide us further, or will you stand with me? Will you cower or fight, brother?"

Kargoth's expression was unreadable, his gaze flicking toward the door as the sounds of battle grew louder. For a moment, Nagar thought he saw a flicker of doubt in the orc's eyes, but then it was gone, replaced by a cold determination.

"We fight," Kargoth said, his voice gruff. "But do not mistake this for acceptance, human. This is merely a matter of survival."

Without another word, Kargoth stormed out of the longhouse, his followers trailing behind him. Nagar exchanged a glance with Irma, a silent acknowledgment of the precarious alliance they had forged. Together, they rushed outside, the chaos of battle unfolding before them.

The village square had become a battleground, human soldiers clashing with the Wontrui orc warriors. The air was thick with the scent of blood and steel, the cries of the wounded mingling with the clash of weapons. Nagar drew his sword, his instincts taking over as he plunged into the fray, Irma at his side. Her bow sang as she loosed arrow after arrow, each finding its mark with deadly precision.

Thok and Grish fought back-to-back, their war hammer and axe a whirlwind of destruction. Princess Vanessa, her face pale but determined, wielded a sword fighting any soldier that Thok knocked down, though Nagar could see the strain in her movements. She was no warrior, but she fought with a ferocity born of desperation.

Amid the chaos, Nagar spotted Kargoth leading a group of Bloodclaw warriors, their boar-tusk headdresses glinting in the torchlight. For now, they fought alongside the Wontrui, their shared enemy forcing them into an uneasy truce. Nagar's heart swelled with a grim hope—perhaps this was the beginning of something greater, a unity forged in the crucible of battle.

But the humans were relentless, their numbers and discipline making up for their lack of familiarity with the terrain. Nagar dodged a swing from a soldier, his sword slicing through the man's armor with a sickening crunch. He had no time to dwell on the life he had taken; another attacker was already upon him.

Out of the corner of his eye, he saw Thok engage a human soldier, the orc's massive frame towering over his opponent. But as Thok raised his hammer for a killing blow, a second soldier emerged from the shadows, his sword aimed at Thok's back.

"Thok!" Vanessa's cry pierced the air, her voice cutting through the chaos.

Without thinking, Nagar lunged forward, intercepting the soldier's strike. Their swords clashed, sparks flying as Nagar's blade met the human's. The soldier was skilled, his movements quick and precise, but Nagar had faced worse. With a swift maneuver, he disarmed the man, sending his sword clattering to the ground.

"Fall back!" Nagar roared, his voice carrying above the din. "Protect the village!"

The Wontrui warriors, recognizing his command, began to retreat, herding the villagers toward the safety of the longhouses. The humans pressed their advantage, but the orcs' knowledge of the terrain gave them an edge. Nagar roared as he lead the group of warriors, each strike a testament to his determination to protect his people.

As the battle raged on, Nagar caught sight of Vanessa, her sword raised to defend Thok as the orc struggled against two attackers. Her face was streaked with dirt, sweat and blood, but her green eyes were blazed with determination. She was no longer the sheltered princess he had first met; she was a survivor, a fighter.

One of the soldiers lunged at Thok, his sword aimed at the orc's heart. Vanessa stepped in front of Thok, her blade intercepting the strike. The force of the blow sent her staggering back, but she held her ground, her grip tightening on the hilt.

"Vanessa, behind you!" Nagar shouted, but it was too late.

The second soldier closed in, his sword raised for a killing blow. Thok, still grappling with his opponent, was unable to intervene. Nagar's heart seized as he saw the blade descend toward Vanessa's back.

In a blur of motion, Vanessa spun, her sword slicing through the air. But the soldier was faster, his blade connecting with her shoulder. Vanessa cried out in pain, her sword slipping from her grasp as she fell to one knee.

Thok roared in fury, shaking off his attacker and turning on the soldier who had struck Vanessa. With a single, powerful swing of his axe, he cleaved through the man's armor, the blow cutting the soldier in half. But the damage was done to Vanessa as her leather armor became drenched in her blood.

Nagar fought his way through the chaos, his mind racing. Vanessa lay on the ground, her face a ghostly white, blood seeping from the wound in her shoulder. Thok knelt beside her, his massive hands gentle as he cradled her head.

"She needs healing," Thok growled, his voice thick with worry.

Nagar nodded, his gaze falling on Irma, who was tending to a wounded orc warrior nearby. "Irma!" he called, his voice cutting through the noise.

Irma looked up, her eyes widening as she saw Vanessa's condition. Without hesitation, she rushed over, her hands glowing with a soft, ethereal light as she began to channel her healing magic. The wound closed slowly, the bleeding stopping as Vanessa's color returned.

"She'll be all right," Irma said, her voice steady despite the chaos around them. "But we need to get her to safety."

Nagar helped Thok lift Vanessa, the orc's strength a stark contrast to the princess's frailty. Together, they carried her toward the longhouse, the battle still raging around them. The Wontrui warriors fought with renewed ferocity, their cries of defiance echoing through the village.

As they reached the longhouse, Nagar turned to survey the battlefield. The humans were retreating, their ranks broken by the orcs' relentless assault. Kargoth stood amidst the chaos, his axe dripping with blood, his expression unreadable. For now, they had held their ground, but Nagar knew this was only the beginning.

Inside the longhouse, Vanessa was laid on a fur-covered bench, her breathing steady but shallow. Irma sat beside her, her hands still glowing as she continued to heal the princess's wounds. Thok stood nearby, his gaze fixed on Vanessa, his expression a mix of worry and gratitude.

Nagar approached Kargoth, who had entered the longhouse moments before. The orc leader's eyes met his, the tension between them palpable.

"We fought well together," Nagar said, his voice low. "Perhaps there is hope for us yet."

Kargoth's lips twisted in a grim smile. "Do not mistake this for loyalty, human. I fight for my people, not for you. But perhaps... perhaps you are not entirely unfit to lead."

Nagar inclined his head, acknowledging the tentative truce. "Then let us build on this. United, we can face whatever comes next."

As the night deepened, the village began to quiet, the wounded tended to, the dead honored. Nagar stood at the entrance of the longhouse, gazing out at the stars twinkling above. The battle had forged a fragile alliance, but the road ahead was uncertain. The humans would return, their greed and ambition unchecked. And within the Wontrui, the seeds of dissent still lingered.

But for now, they had survived. And in survival, there was hope.

Nagar turned back to the longhouse, his gaze falling on Irma, who sat beside Vanessa, her hand resting gently on the princess's forehead. Thok stood nearby, his massive frame a silent guardian. Together, they were a family, bound by shared trials and a common purpose.

The journey was far from over, but Nagar knew they would face it together. And in that knowledge, he found the strength to lead, to protect, and to hope for a future where humans and orcs could stand side by side, not as enemies, but as allies.

As the night deepened, the village settled into an uneasy peace. However Nagar knew that the true test lay ahead, in the battles yet to come and the alliances yet to be forged. For now, they had survived. And in survival, there was hope.

Chapter 11

The air was thick with the scent of charred wood and damp earth as the orcs, Nagar, Irma, and Princess Vanessa gathered amidst the ruins of the Wontrui village. The once-vibrant settlement now lay in shambles, its structures reduced to smoldering remnants of what had been a thriving community. The silence was heavy, broken only by the occasional crackle of dying flames and the distant cries of wounded creatures. The weight of their losses pressed upon them, but amidst the devastation, a new resolve began to take shape.

Princess Vanessa stood tall, her regal bearing undiminished despite the grime, blood, and soot that clung to her leather armor and blonde hair. Her appearance was far from the one she once had months ago. Her green eyes, sharp and determined, scanned the faces of those around her. "My father won't stop," she said, her voice steady but laced with a deep, abiding sorrow. "He'll send his entire army to wipe you out. He'll never rest until every last orc is gone." Her words hung in the air, a grim reminder of the relentless threat they faced.

Nagar, his broad shoulders squared and his hands still smeared with ash from the search and rescue attempts from the aftermath of the battle, shook his head. "He can't do that," he said, his voice gruff but firm. "There are women and children here. It's not just warriors. What he wants to do is genocide." His gaze swept over the gathered orcs, his expression a mix of defiance and protectiveness. "I won't let him destroy what these orcs have built for centuries."

Thok, his massive frame looming like a mountain, crossed his arms and scowled. "Then we bring the fight to him," he growled, pounding his chest. "We strike first. Show him what happens when he fucks with the orcs." His words were met with murmurs of agreement from the other orcs, their battle-hardened spirits stirring at the prospect of retaliation.

Irma, her elven features serene but her eyes sharp with intelligence, shook her head. "Two orc clans aren't enough to defeat the green kingdom," she said, her voice calm but firm. "We need more. We need to recruit others to our cause. Alone, we're strong, but together, we're unstoppable." Her gaze met Nagar's, and for a moment, the unspoken bond between them seemed to strengthen, a silent acknowledgment of the path ahead.

Kargoth'a brow furrowed, his skepticism evident. "And what's in it for the other orcs? Why should they risk their lives for us? What do they gain from this fight?" His question hung in the air, a challenge that demanded a compelling answer.

Princess Vanessa stepped forward, her eyes burning with a fierce determination. "They'll earn their freedom," she declared, her voice ringing with conviction. "If we defeat my father, I'll claim my throne. As queen of the kingdom, I swear to never raise a sword against the orcs. All creatures will be considered equals. No more oppression, no more fear. We'll build a kingdom where everyone has a place."

Her words struck a chord deep within the hearts of the orcs. For generations, they had been hunted, enslaved, and marginalized. The promise of freedom—true, unfettered freedom—was a dream they had long thought impossible. Hope flickered in their eyes, a fragile but growing flame. Many began to murmur and nod in agreement.

Nagar nodded, a rare smile tugging at his lips. "Then it's settled," he said, his voice steady. "We'll send out envoys to recruit other orcs. There are clans scattered across these lands, each with their own grievances against the Green Kingdom. If we show them what's at stake, they'll join us."

Irma added, her voice thoughtful, "And we should seek the help of the elves. They've long been allies of nature and freedom. If they see a chance for a world where all creatures are equal, they'll stand with us."

"Aye, good plan." Nagar grinned.

"We will need more than orcs and elves. If we are to win the hearts of the kingdom, we must win this war with humans too." Vanessa added.

"Who will join this cause?" Thok asked.

"I know of those who are still loyal to me. Knights and soldiers who don't believe in my father's racist thoughts and will follow me into battle. I could convince some to join us."

"You will not travel alone, not with your father trying to kill you. I will accompany you as your guard." Thok bowed.

Vanessa smiled and bowed, "thank you Thok." Two held a lingering gazed before looking away.

Irma and Nagar shared a knowing glance before Irma spoke up. "I will travel the the elven territory. I know those lands best and if I am among the group, you'd less likely be attacked on sight."

"I'm coming with you." Nagar added.

Kargoth nodded, and crossed his arms. "I will organize envoys to go to the other orc villages. We will spread the word and invite any orc worthy of holding a blade."

"Then it's settled. Get some rest tonight everyone as tomorrow we set off to war."

The group fell silent as they broke apart, each lost in their own thoughts as they considered the enormity of the task before them. The road ahead would be fraught with danger, but the promise of a better future—a future where no one would be oppressed again—was worth the risk.

As the sun began to set, casting long shadows across the ruined village, the orcs began to stir. They moved with purpose, their earlier despair replaced by a newfound sense of determination. Envoys were chosen, brave warriors who would carry their message to distant clans. Plans were made to seek out the elusive elves, to plead their case and forge an alliance.

Nagar and Irma stood apart from the others, their shoulders brushing as they watched the orcs prepare. "Do you think it'll work?" Irma asked, her voice soft but laced with doubt. "Convincing the elves, finding human allies, uniting the orcs... it's a lot to ask."

Nagar turned to her, his gaze steady. "It's our only chance," he said simply. "We can't let the Green Kingdom win. Not when so much is at stake." He reached out, his hand brushing hers, a silent reassurance that they were in this together.

Irma smiled, a small but genuine expression of gratitude. "Then we'll make it work," she said, her voice firm. "Together."

"Together," he grinned leaning in to give her a lingering kiss.

Chapter 12

The fire crackled softly, its flames dancing like wild spirits, casting an amber glow over the makeshift camp. Nagar and Irma sat close, their bodies pressed together, the warmth of the fire mingling with the heat of their shared dreams. The ale in their mugs was strong, its bitterness a stark contrast to the sweetness of their whispered plans. They spoke of revolution, of a world where all creatures—orcs, elves, humans, and more—could live free from oppression. It was a dream that felt both impossibly distant and achingly close, fueled by the fire in their hearts and the bond between them.

Irma leaned into Nagar, her head resting on his shoulder, her voice soft but resolute. "You're going to be a great leader," she said, a playful smile tugging at her lips. "Remember when you thought you couldn't do it?" Nagar chuckled, his hand brushing her hair, the strands felt like silk against his dark calloused fingertips.

"I'm just happy I have you," he murmured, his voice thick with emotion. "I love you." Irma's smile widened, and she pressed a tender kiss to his lips. It was a kiss filled with promise, with the weight of everything they had been through and everything they hoped to achieve.

They pulled apart, their bodies still entwined, and continued to cuddle, the fire casting a golden glow over them. Nearby, Princess Vanessa and Thok sat close, their laughter mingling with the crackle of the fire. They shared a flask of ale, their bodies pressed together as they whispered and giggled. Vanessa's hand rested on Thok's arm, and he pulled her closer, their lips meeting in a passionate kiss. The sight was both endearing and amusing, a reminder that even in the midst of chaos, love and desire could flourish.

Irma and Nagar exchanged amused glances, watching as the pair rose and disappeared into Thok's hut. "Looks like the princess has a thing for Orcs," Irma remarked with a grin.

"I didn't think she'd fall for one, especially considering she was kidnapped by an orc..." Nagar added.

"Well, considering the looks that she gave Thok, I'm not surprised. Thok is nothing like that brute Oz."

"True," Nagar laughed, nodding in agreement. Moments later, distant moans drifted through the air, and they shared a knowing chuckle. "Well, I don't need to guess what they're up to," Nagar said, his tone light. Irma's eyes sparkled as she turned to him. "Listening to them is making me... restless," she admitted, her voice low, her cheeks flushed with a mixture of embarrassment and desire.

Nagar's grin widened, and he took her hand, his touch firm and reassuring. "Perhaps we should do something about that," he suggested, his voice a low rumble that sent a shiver down her spine. He led her to their hut, the furs inside soft and inviting. The air was cool, but the warmth of their bodies and the fire outside seemed to envelop them, creating a cocoon of intimacy.

Inside, they moved with urgency, their passion ignited by the night's energy. Nagar's hands were everywhere, his touch both gentle and demanding as he pulled her close. Their lips met in a fierce kiss, their tongues tangling in a dance as old as time. Irma's hands gripped his shoulders, her nails digging into his skin as she pressed herself against him, her body aching for his.

Their clothes were discarded quickly, falling to the floor in a forgotten heap. Nagar's eyes roamed over her body, his gaze hungry yet tender. Her petite slender frame, her beige skin glowing in the dim light, contrasted beautifully with his dark, muscular form. He cupped her small soft breast in his hand and sucked on her tit. She tilted her head back as his tongue swirled around her sensitive hard nipple.

As they kissed, he positioned her on all fours, his hands gripping her hips, his thumbs brushing the curve of her ass. Irma trembled from his touch. The contrast of her skin against his palms sent a thrill through him, a reminder of the raw, primal desire that pulsed between them.

"You're so beautiful," he murmured, his breath hot against her neck. Irma shivered; her body already damp with anticipation. "I need you," she whispered, her voice trembling.

Nagar didn't make her wait. He entered her from behind, his thick black cock filling her completely, stretching her in a way that made her moan softly. The sensation was intoxicating, his size a perfect fit for her tightness, his hardness a stark contrast to her softness. He held her hips firmly, his hands never leaving her, as he began to thrust. Each movement was deliberate, steady, his breath coming in short gasps as he relished the feel of her body around him.

"Fuck, Irma," he groaned, his voice rough with need. "You feel so good."

Irma's head fell back, her hair cascading over her shoulders as she arched her back, meeting his thrusts with her own. As her tits swayed with every powerful thrust, she moaned as he split her in two with his large cock.

"Harder," she demanded, her voice a plea. "Fuck me harder, Nagar."

He obliged, his thrusts becoming more urgent, more primal. His hands gripped her ass tighter, his fingers digging into her flesh as he pounded into her, the sound of their bodies slapping together filling the small hut. The air was thick with the scent of their desire, the sweat on their skin, the musky aroma of their arousal.

"Oh, fuck," Irma moaned, her voice breaking as she felt the coil of pleasure tightening within her. "I'm close, Nagar. Don't stop. Don't stop. Don't...ugh...."

Nagar growled, his thrusts becoming almost frantic as he chased his own release. "Come for me, baby," he urged, his voice a low growl. "Let me feel you squeeze my cock."

Irma's body trembled as she climaxed, her walls clenching around him, milking him in a rhythm that drove him wild. "Fuck, Yes!" she cried out, her voice a mix of pleasure and desperation. "Nagar, I'm—I'm cumming!"

Her orgasm was a tidal wave, crashing over her in waves of ecstasy. Nagar followed moments later, his own release explosive, his cock pulsing deep within her as he filled her with his seed. "Irma," he groaned, his voice a ragged whisper as he collapsed on top of her, his body trembling with the force of his climax.

They lay there for a moment, their hearts pounding, their breaths coming in ragged gasps. Nagar rolled onto his side, pulling Irma into his arms, his hand stroking her hair gently. "I love you," he whispered, his lips brushing her forehead.

Irma smiled, her body still buzzing with the aftermath of their passion. "I love you too," she replied, her voice soft and content. She snuggled closer, her head resting on his chest, the steady beat of his heart a soothing rhythm.

Outside, the fire continued to crackle, its flames casting flickering shadows on the walls of the hut. The distant sounds of the night—the rustle of leaves, the occasional hoot of an owl—were a reminder of the world beyond their small sanctuary. But for now, they were lost in each other, their bodies and souls intertwined in a way that made the rest of the world fade away.

Nagar's fingers traced lazy patterns on her bare back, his touch gentle and reassuring. "We're going to make this work," he murmured, his voice filled with determination. "We're going to free them all, Irma. I promise."

Irma nodded, her eyes drifting closed as she listened to the steady rhythm of his heart. "I know we will," she whispered. "Together, we can do anything."

They lay there in silence, the warmth of their bodies and the promise of their shared dream keeping the chill of the night at bay. The future was uncertain, filled with challenges and dangers they couldn't yet imagine. But in that moment, with Nagar's arms around her and the sound of his heartbeat lulling her into a peaceful slumber, Irma felt a sense of hope she hadn't known in a long time.

The fire outside continued to burn, its flames a beacon of warmth and light in the darkness. And inside the hut, Nagar and Irma held each other close, their love a flame that would not be extinguished, no matter what the future held. The night deepened, and the world outside seemed to hold its breath, as if waiting to see what the dawn would bring. But for now, in the stillness of their embrace, everything was right. Everything was perfect.

Chapter 13

The morning sun filtered through the canopy of the ancient woods, casting dappled light on the forest floor as Nagar and Irma made their way deeper into the elven territory. The air was thick with the scent of pine and damp earth, and the rustling of leaves beneath their boots was the only sound breaking the forest's serene silence. Nagar's broad shoulders moved with a steady rhythm, his sword sheathed at his side, while Irma's slender frame glided effortlessly beside him, her bow slung across her back. The weight of their mission hung between them, but there was also a quiet hope—a hope for a future beyond the war.

"If we win this," Nagar began, his voice low and steady, "I can see a life with you. A real one. Before all of this, I saw my life as a free sell sword, but now all I want to do is hold you and live a long life in your arms. I want a place to call our own, a place where we can make love all day and have children. A place that is way from war and death. Its quiet and just for us. Would you like that?" His words hung in the air, heavy with meaning. He glanced at Irma, his dark eyes searching hers for a reaction. The forest seemed to hold its breath.

Irma's gaze softened, her eyes reflecting the light filtering through the trees. She nodded, her voice barely above a whisper. "Yes, I would. I want all of those things. As long as I have you, I'm happy." Her words were simple, yet they carried the weight of a promise—a promise of a future they both desperately wanted but dared not take for granted.

They walked in silence for a while, the only sound the crunch of leaves and the distant chirping of birds. The forest was alive around them, its ancient trees standing as silent witnesses to their journey. Nagar's mind wandered to the battles they had fought, the sacrifices they had made, and the uncertain path ahead. But for the first time in a long while, he allowed himself to imagine a life beyond the war—a life with Irma.

Irma's thoughts mirrored his own. She thought of the nights they had shared, the moments of tenderness amidst the chaos, and the unspoken bond that had grown between them. She had always valued her freedom, but with Nagar, she felt a different kind of liberation—a freedom to be herself, to love without fear.

As they walked, the forest began to change. The trees grew taller, their branches intertwining to form a natural archway. The air grew cooler, and the scent of pine gave way to the sweet fragrance of blooming flowers. They were nearing the elven encampment, a place few outsiders had ever seen.

The first sign of the settlement was a faint hum of activity—the soft murmur of voices, the clinking of tools, and the occasional laughter of children. As they emerged from the thicket, the encampment revealed itself in all its splendor. Nestled within a clearing, the elven village was a masterpiece of harmony with nature. Treehouses crafted from living wood rose gracefully among the branches, their surfaces adorned with intricate carvings of leaves and vines. Bridges made of woven vines connected the platforms, while lanterns filled with glowing fireflies provided a soft, ethereal light.

The elves themselves were a sight to behold. Their skin glowed with an otherworldly luminescence, their hair shimmering in hues of silver, gold, and emerald. They moved with a grace that seemed almost magical, their eyes sharp and wise. As Nagar and Irma entered the clearing, all activity ceased, and every pair of eyes turned toward them.

Irma stepped forward, her presence commanding despite her petite frame. She raised her hands in a gesture of peace, her voice clear and steady. "We come in friendship, seeking your aid." She spoke in her native elvish tongue.

The elves exchanged wary glances, their expressions a mix of curiosity and suspicion. Their leader, a tall elf with silver hair and eyes that seemed to see right through one's soul, stepped forward. "There is no need to us our native language, outsider," he spat in human form. "Speak your purpose," he said, his voice like the rustling of leaves.

Irma and Nagar shared a look before she stepped forward and took a deep breath, her gaze sweeping over the gathered elves. "We are fighting against King Hector, a tyrant who has oppressed not just humans, but orcs and elves alike. If we succeed, we can end his reign of terror. Queen Vanessa, who stands with us, has promised a new era of equality—a world where no one is treated as a second-class citizen. With your help, we can make this vision a reality."

The elves murmured among themselves, their voices a mix of hope and skepticism. The leader raised a hand for silence, his eyes never leaving Irma's. "Why should we trust you? Humans have betrayed us before."

Nagar stepped forward, his presence commanding respect. "Because this time, it's not just humans fighting. It's a coalition of all races—orcs, elves, and humans united against a common enemy. We've seen the cost of division, and we're willing to pay the price for unity."

The leader studied them both, his expression unreadable. After a long moment, he nodded. "Very well. We will hear your plea. But know this: the elves do not give their allegiance lightly."

He motioned for them to follow, and they were led to a central platform where the elders of the encampment gathered. The air was thick with tension as Irma and Nagar stood before them, their fates hanging in the balance.

Irma spoke first, her words passionate yet measured. "King Hector's tyranny knows no bounds. He has slaughtered orcs, enslaved elves, and oppressed his own people. But we have a chance to change that. With your help, we can bring down his regime and build a new world—a world where every being, regardless of race, is treated with dignity and respect."

Nagar added, his voice steady and resolute. "We've already begun to unite the orc clans. With your magic, your knowledge of the forest, and your skill in battle, we can turn the tide of this war. Together, we are unstoppable."

The elders conferred in hushed tones, their voices a mix of elvish and common tongue. The wait was agonizing, but finally, the leader stepped forward once more. "We will join you," he declared, his voice carrying across the clearing. "But understand this: we fight not for humans, nor for orcs, but for the freedom of all beings. If Queen Vanessa fails to keep her promise, she will answer to us."

A wave of relief washed over Nagar and Irma, but it was tempered by the gravity of the responsibility they now carried. They had secured the elves' alliance, but the true test lay ahead—winning the war and building the world they had promised.

As the sun dipped below the horizon, casting the forest in hues of orange and purple, Nagar and Irma stood side by side, gazing out at the elven encampment. The lanterns had been lit, their soft glow illuminating the treehouses and bridges like a constellation of stars. The elves moved about their tasks with renewed purpose, their voices a harmonious melody in the evening air.

"We're really doing this," Irma murmured, her hand finding Nagar's.

Nagar squeezed her hand, his gaze steady. "We are. And we're not doing it alone."

In the distance, the forest whispered secrets of ancient battles and forgotten alliances. But for Nagar and Irma, the future was theirs to shape—a future of unity, freedom, and love. The path ahead was uncertain, but together, they would face whatever came their way.

The alliance was sealed, and the path to freedom grew clearer. But the war was far from over, and the true test of their resolve lay ahead. As the stars began to twinkle in the night sky, Nagar and Irma stood at the threshold of a new chapter, their hearts filled with hope and their spirits unyielding. The forest's embrace was both a sanctuary and a reminder—a reminder that the fight for freedom was worth every sacrifice.

And so, under the watchful gaze of the ancient woods, they prepared for the battles to come, their bond stronger than ever, their purpose unshakable. The world they envisioned was within reach, and they would stop at nothing to make it a reality.

Chapter 14

The night air was thick with anticipation as the diverse assembly of elves, orcs, and humans loyal to Princess Vanessa's cause gathered beneath the starry sky. The ancient woods, once a place of whispered secrets and hidden dangers, now echoed with the sounds of unity and hope. Torches flickered, casting dancing shadows on the faces of the crowd, their eyes gleaming with determination and fear. At the center of it all stood Princess Vanessa, her presence commanding yet gentle, her voice steady as she addressed the multitude. She was dressed not in robes, but thick leather armor with a sword tied on her waist. She was no longer the weak princess that Nagar rescued, but a warrior ready to fight for what she believed in.

"My friends," she began, her words carrying across the clearing like a soothing balm, "tonight we stand together, not as elves, orcs, or humans, but as a single force united against tyranny. I thank each and every one of you for your unwavering loyalty and courage. We have come too far to turn back now. We fight not just for ourselves, but for the freedom of all who will come after us."

Her gaze swept across the crowd, lingering on the faces of those who had sacrificed so much. She smiled at Thok, her orcish companion, his massive frame standing tall beside her. Their bond was more than a political alliance; it was a symbol of the unity she hoped to achieve. "As your new queen," she continued, her voice firm, "my first act will be to defend the freedom of every being in this land. Malice toward another race will not be tolerated. Those who seek to divide us will face the harshest of penalties. We will build a future where no one lives in fear of their neighbor."

The crowd murmured in approval, their nods and whispers a testament to their shared vision. Vanessa's smile widened as she took Thok's hand, holding it up for all to see. "My second act as queen will be to ensure that peace among our races endures for generations. That is why I will marry Thok. Our children, will be half orc and half human, and will be the living embodiment of the unity we strive for. They will grow up in a world where all children, regardless of their blood, are treated as equals."

The clearing erupted in cheers, the sound deafening as orcs, elves, and humans alike raised their voices in celebration. Vanessa's heart swelled with pride and hope. She squeezed Thok's hand, her eyes meeting his in a silent promise. "So tonight," she called out, her voice rising above the din, "eat, drink, and fuck. Live like there's no tomorrow, for tomorrow we march toward a new future!"

The crowd roared its approval, the tension of the past weeks melting away in the face of their shared purpose. Music began to play, the rhythmic beat of drums and the melodic hum of elven flutes weaving together in a harmony that mirrored the unity of the gathering. Drinks were passed around, and laughter filled the air as old enemies became allies, their differences set aside in the face of a common goal.

Vanessa turned to Thok, her smile soft as she kissed him gently. "How was the speech?" she asked, her voice low.

Thok grinned, his tusks gleaming in the torchlight. "You spoke true words, my queen. They will follow you to the ends of the earth."

Nearby, Nagar and Irma stood watching, their hands clasped tightly. Nagar's dark skin contrasted sharply with Irma's beige, elven complexion, their bond a quiet testament to the unity Vanessa had spoken of. "She did well," Nagar murmured, his voice filled with pride.

Irma nodded, her eyes shining with admiration. "She has a way with words. And with people."

Vanessa approached them, her expression warm. "What did you think?" she asked, her tone light.

"It was perfect," Irma replied without hesitation. "You gave them hope."

"Good," Vanessa said, her smile widening. "Now, go enjoy yourselves. Tomorrow, we march to the castle and win this war."

With a final nod, Vanessa took Thok's hand, and the two disappeared into his hut, leaving Nagar and Irma alone amidst the revelry. The air was thick with the scent of sweat, ale, and desire as the celebration continued around them. Nagar turned to Irma, his eyes dark with unspoken emotion. "Come," he said, his voice rough. "Let's go."

They retreated to their own hut, the furs laid out on the floor inviting and warm. The world outside seemed to fade away as they shed their clothes, their bodies glistening in the dim light of the single torch that flickered in the corner. Nagar's muscles rippled as he moved, his dark skin a stark contrast to Irma's pale, delicate frame. They lay down together, their lips meeting in a kiss that was both tender and hungry, their tongues tangling in a dance as old as time.

Nagar's hands roamed over Irma's body, his touch reverent as he traced the curves of her breasts, the dip of her waist, the swell of her hips. Irma moaned softly, her fingers digging into his shoulders as she pulled him closer. "Nagar," she whispered, her voice thick with desire. "I need you."

He smiled against her skin, his breath hot as he kissed his way down her body. "Always," he murmured, his lips brushing against her ear. "You are my everything, Irma. My strength, my heart, my soul."

His mouth found her breast, his tongue swirling around her dark perked nipple as he teased and sucked, his hands cupping her fullness. Irma arched her back, her moans filling the small space as pleasure coiled low in her belly. "Nagar," she gasped, her fingers threading through his hair. "Please."

He chuckled, the vibration sending shivers through her. "Impatient, my love?" he teased, his lips trailing down her stomach, his tongue dipping into her navel. "I'm just getting started."

His mouth continued its journey southward, his breath ghosting over her sensitive skin as he kissed his way lower. Irma's breath hitched as his lips brushed against the junction of her thighs, his tongue flicking teasingly before he spread her legs and settled between them. His hands gripped her hips, holding her steady as he delved deeper, his tongue lapping at her wetness, his fingers probing her entrance.

"Oh, fuck," Irma moaned, her head falling back as pleasure washed over her. Nagar's mouth was relentless, his tongue and fingers working in perfect harmony as he drove her higher and higher. Her body trembled, her muscles tightening as she teetered on the edge of release. "Nagar, I—"

"Let go, my love," he murmured against her skin, his voice a rumble that vibrated through her. "Give it to me."

Irma cried out, her body convulsing as she surrendered to the pleasure, her juices flooding Nagar's mouth. He drank her in, his tongue lapping at her greedily as he savored her taste, his fingers continuing to stroke her through her orgasm until she was boneless and breathless beneath him.

When she finally came down, Nagar kissed his way back up her body, his lips brushing against her skin as he smiled down at her. "Better?" he asked, his voice husky.

Irma laughed, her hand reaching up to cup his cheek. "Much," she admitted, her voice soft. "But now it's my turn."

She rolled him onto his back, her hands tracing the contours of his body as she explored him with reverence. His black cock stood proud and thick, his length straining as he watched her with dark, hungry eyes. Irma's mouth watered as she took him in her hand, her fingers stroking his length as she leaned down to kiss the head of his cock, her tongue flicking against the tiny sensitive slit.

Nagar groaned, his hands gripping the furs as he fought for control. "Irma," he warned, his voice thick with need. "If you keep that up, I won't last."

She smiled against his skin, her lips wrapping around the head of his cock as she took him into her mouth. Her tongue swirled around him, her hand pumping his length in time with her movements as she sucked him deep, her cheeks hollowing as she took him as far as she could.

"Fuck," Nagar gasped, his hips bucking involuntarily as pleasure surged through him. Irma's mouth was hot and wet, her lips and tongue driving him wild as she worked him with skill and enthusiasm. He tangled his fingers in her hair, his thighs tensing as he fought to hold back, to make this last.

But Irma was relentless, her mouth and hand working in perfect sync as she drove him higher and higher. Her other hand reached down to stroke his balls, her fingers massaging him as she sucked him deep, her tongue flicking against the sensitive underside of his cock.

"Irma," Nagar groaned, his voice a warning. "I'm close."

She hummed her response, the vibration sending him over the edge. Nagar cried out, his body tensing as he came, his cock pulsing in Irma's mouth as she swallowed him down, her hand milking him dry. She sucked him clean, her lips brushing against his sensitive skin as she smiled up at him.

"Better?" she asked, her voice teasing.

Nagar laughed, his hand reaching up to tug her down beside him. "Much," he admitted, his voice hoarse. "You're incredible."

They lay together, their bodies glistening with sweat, their hearts pounding in unison. Irma snuggled into Nagar's side, her head resting on his chest as she listened to the steady beat of his heart. Outside, the celebration continued, the sounds of laughter and music filtering through the walls of the hut.

Nagar stroked Irma's hair, his fingers threading through the black silk like strands as he held her close. "Irma," he began, his voice soft but resolute. "There's something I need to ask you."

She looked up at him, her eyes curious. "What is it?"

He took a deep breath, his heart pounding in his chest. "Marry me," he said, his voice steady despite the turmoil within him. "Be my wife, my partner, my everything. Face this world with me, side by side, for the rest of our lives."

Irma's eyes widened, tears welling up as she stared at him. "Nagar," she whispered, her voice thick with emotion. "Are you sure? After everything—"

"I've never been more sure of anything in my life," he interrupted, his voice firm. "You are my home, Irma. My sanctuary. My reason for fighting. Marry me, and let's build a future together, no matter what comes our way."

Irma's tears spilled over, her hands reaching up to cup his face as she kissed him fiercely. "Yes," she whispered against his lips. "Yes, Nagar. I'll marry you. I love you more than anything."

He smiled, his heart swelling with joy as he pulled her into his arms, holding her close. Outside, the night continued, the world moving on as it always did. But in that moment, in that small hut amidst the ancient woods, Nagar and Irma found their own piece of forever, their love a beacon of hope in a world filled with darkness.

As they lay entwined, their bodies still warm from their passion, they listened to the sounds of the celebration, the laughter and music a reminder of the unity they had helped to forge. Tomorrow, they would march to the castle, ready to face whatever challenges lay ahead. But for now, in the quiet of their hut, they had each other, their love a promise of a brighter future.

The night deepened, the stars shining brightly above as the world slept, unaware of the quiet revolution taking place within the hearts of those who dared to dream of a better tomorrow. And in that stillness, Nagar and Irma found their peace, their love a testament to the power of unity and the strength of the human—and elven—spirit.

The story of their love, like the tale of their journey, was far from over. But for now, in the quiet of the night, they rested, their hearts full, their futures intertwined, ready to face whatever came next, together.

Chapter 15

The air above the fields of the Green Kingdom shimmered with tension, as if the very heavens held their breath in anticipation of the clash to come. The combined forces of elves, orcs, and loyal humans stood united, their banners snapping in the brisk autumn wind. The elf standards, adorned with silver leaves and stars, fluttered alongside the rugged orcish banners, marked with jagged claws and blood-red symbols. Human flags, bearing the emblem of the rising sun, completed the tapestry of defiance. Together, they formed a mosaic of hope and resistance, a testament to the fragile alliance forged in the fires of shared oppression.

At the forefront of this diverse army stood Nagar, his presence commanding yet unassuming. His leather armor, gleamed in the morning light. Beside him, Irma's grace and poise belied the power she held within. Her bow, crafted from the heartwood of an ancient oak, rested across her back, while her quiver brimmed with arrows tipped with red feathers. Behind them, Princess Vanessa and Thok stood side by side, their bond a living symbol of the unity they sought to achieve. Vanessa's resolve was etched into every line of her face, while Thok's towering form exuded a quiet strength, his war-hammer slung across his broad shoulders.

Across the field, King Hector's army awaited, a sea of steel and malice. Hector himself sat atop his warhorse, his armor polished to a blinding sheen, his crown glinting like a mockery of the light. His green eyes, cold and calculating, fixed on his daughter with a mixture of hatred and disdain. The silence between the two armies was palpable, broken only by the occasional clank of armor and the distant cries of birds fleeing the impending storm.

Hector spurred his horse forward, stopping just within earshot of the alliance's lines. His gaze locked onto Vanessa, and his lips curled into a snarl. "You are no daughter of mine. When I kill you and your army, I will erase your name from the history books. The mere mention of you will be punishable by death," he spat, his voice carrying across the field like a blade. The words struck Vanessa like a physical blow, but her expression remained steadfast.

"You lost the right to call me that the moment you tried to kill me," Vanessa replied, her voice steady and cold. "That's when I saw your true nature. A tyrant, a murderer, a man who would slaughter his own blood to cling to power."

Hector's face darkened, his eyes blazing with fury. He leaned forward in his saddle, spitting at her feet. "I hope you die a slow, agonizing death," he growled. "May the ground reject your bones, the heavens deny you peace, and the fires of hell burn you for eternity."

Vanessa's gaze never wavered. "Your words mean nothing to me," she said. "But know this: today, your reign ends. Not by my hand, but by the hands of those you've oppressed. By the hands of a kingdom that will no longer bow to your cruelty."

Hector's laughter was harsh, bitter. "Dreams of fools," he sneered. "You think a rabble of elves, orcs, and traitors can stand against me? You'll all be dead by sunset." With that, he wheeled his horse around and rode back to his troops, leaving the air thick with the weight of his malice.

The silence that followed was heavy, broken only by the sound of commanders rallying their troops. Nagar stepped forward, his presence a beacon of calm amidst the storm. He raised his sword, its blade catching the sunlight, and his voice rang out, clear and strong.

"Today, we fight not just for victory, but for justice!" he declared. "For Vanessa, who dared to stand against tyranny! For the elves, who have endured centuries of scorn! For the orcs, who have been driven from their homes! For the humans who refuse to kneel to a tyrant! Today, we fight for the future of the Green Kingdom—a future built on equality, on unity, on hope!"

His words ignited a fire in the hearts of the alliance. Cheers erupted, a chorus of determination and defiance. Nagar's gaze swept across the ranks, meeting the eyes of Irma, Vanessa, and Thok. In that moment, they were more than leaders; they were symbols of a dream worth dying for.

With a roar that shook the earth, Nagar led the charge. His sword flashed in the sunlight as he surged forward, the alliance following in his wake. The ground trembled beneath the weight of their advance, the air filled with battle cries and the clash of steel.

The battle was a maelstrom of chaos and carnage. Arrows darkened the sky, each one a messenger of death. Swords clashed, shields shattered, and the ground ran red with blood. The elves fought with precision, their movements graceful yet deadly. The orcs, with their brute strength and unwavering ferocity, carved a path through the enemy lines. The humans, loyal and resolute, held the center, their formation unyielding.

Irma moved like a specter of death, her bow singing as she loosed arrow after arrow with unerring accuracy. Each shot found its mark, striking down enemy commanders and breaking their lines. Her magic, a subtle yet potent force, wove through the battlefield, healing the wounded and bolstering the weary.

Thok was a force of nature, his war-hammer crushing armor and bone alike. He fought with a ferocity born of centuries of oppression, each blow a testament to the suffering of his people. Yet, amidst the chaos, he never lost sight of Vanessa, his presence a silent promise of protection.

Vanessa, though untrained in the ways of war, fought with a resolve that inspired those around her. Her strikes were not those of a warrior, but of a woman fighting for her people, for her future, for her very soul.

Nagar was the heart of the battle, his sword a whirlwind of steel and fury. He moved with a purpose, his every action calculated yet driven by passion. He fought not just for victory, but for the dream he and Irma had nurtured—a dream of a world where love and justice could flourish.

The battle raged on, relentless and unforgiving. Lives were lost on both sides, the field littered with the fallen. Yet, the alliance fought with a determination that could not be broken. Slowly, inexorably, they began to gain the upper hand.

Hector, sensing the tide turning, rallied his troops with a ferocity born of desperation. He charged into the fray, his sword cleaving through the ranks of the alliance. His eyes, wild with rage, sought out Vanessa, but she was protected by a wall of her allies.

Nagar, seeing the king's intent, broke through the enemy lines with a roar. His path was a trail of destruction, each strike bringing him closer to Hector. The two clashed in a duel that seemed to freeze time itself. Their swords met in a shower of sparks, each blow echoing across the battlefield.

Hector was a formidable foe, his skill honed by decades of war. But Nagar fought with the strength of a man who had nothing left to lose, who had found love and purpose in a world that had once offered him only despair. With a final, powerful strike, Nagar's sword pierced Hector's armor, finding its mark.

The king staggered, his eyes widening in disbelief. He fell to his knees, his sword slipping from his grasp. Nagar stood over him, his chest heaving, his sword still stained with the king's blood.

"It ends here," Nagar said, his voice low and steady. "Your reign of terror is over."

Hector's lips twisted into a grim smile. "You may have won the battle," he rasped, "but you'll never hold this kingdom. The people will never accept you."

Nagar's expression hardened. "They will accept Vanessa," he said. "And through her, they will learn to accept each other."

With that, Hector's head fell forward, his life slipping away. The battlefield fell silent, the only sound the ragged breathing of the survivors. The remaining troops of the Green Kingdom, seeing their king fallen, knelt in submission. Their loyalty, once unwavering, now shifted to the rightful heir.

Vanessa stepped forward, her gaze sweeping across the field. Her expression was one of sorrow, not triumph. She had lost a father, but gained a kingdom. She raised her hands, her voice carrying across the silence.

"This war was not fought for conquest, but for justice," she said. "For the right of every being, regardless of race or creed, to live in peace and equality. Today, we begin the hard work of rebuilding—of forging a kingdom where all are welcome, where all are valued."

One by one, the elves, orcs, and humans bowed their heads. Nagar stepped forward, his voice echoing across the field. "Long live Queen Vanessa," he declared.

The cry was taken up by all, a chorus of hope and renewal. Vanessa ascended the throne, her reign beginning amidst the ashes of war. But as she looked out upon the field, her heart was heavy. The road ahead would be long and fraught with challenges. Yet, standing beside Nagar, Irma, and Thok, she knew they would face it together.

The sun dipped below the horizon, casting the battlefield in a golden light. The air was thick with the scent of blood and smoke, but also with the promise of a new beginning. The story of the Green Kingdom was far from over, its pages still unwritten. And as the stars began to twinkle in the night sky, the alliance stood united, ready to face whatever the future held.

For in the end, it was not just a kingdom they had saved, but a dream—a dream of unity, of love, of a world where all could stand together, strong and free. And in that dream, there was hope—hope for a future where the bonds of friendship and love could overcome even the darkest of nights.

Chapter 16

In the wake of the great battle, the air still carried the faint scent of smoke and the echoes of clashing steel. The once-bloodied fields of the Green Kingdom now lay quiet, the earth slowly healing under the gentle touch of the morning sun.

Standing in the throne room, Queen Vanessa, her crown resting lightly upon her brow, wearing a white gown smiled at her subjects. Her heart was heavy with the weight of loss but buoyed by the promise of a new beginning. The kingdom would rise again, not as a realm of tyranny and division, but as a beacon of unity and justice.

Among the victors, Nagar and Irma stood apart, their presence commanding yet unassuming. Nagar, once a dangerous sell sword, now stood as a hero of Green Kingdom, his broad shoulders squared with the weight of his new title. He was adorned with metals of his heroics and wore freshly tailored clothes.

Irma, despite her elven heritage was now know for her heroism, and not her appearance. She had removed her armor and adorned herself in the finest silk in the kingdom and stood by Nagar's side, her almond-shaped eyes reflecting the dawn's light with a warmth that seemed to illuminate the world around her. Together, they were a testament to the power of love and resilience, their bond unbreakable even in the face of war.

Queen Vanessa approached them, her steps measured and deliberate. Her voice, though soft, carried an authority that commanded attention. "Nagar, Irma," she began, her eyes filled with gratitude and respect. "Your bravery and loyalty have not gone unnoticed. The kingdom owes you a debt that can never be fully repaid. As a token of my esteem, I bestow upon you the titles of Lord and Lady of the Western Isles. These lands once belonged to men loyal to my father, but that was a different time now. The castle, the land it sits on, and its people are all yours to rule as you see fit. May they prosper under your care, as you have prospered in the face of adversity."

Nagar bowed his head, his hand resting briefly on the hilt of his sword before he spoke. "Your Majesty, we are humbled by your generosity. The Western Isles shall be a testament to the ideals we fought for—unity, justice, and peace."

Irma, her voice steady and clear, added, "We shall honor this gift, Your Majesty and we shall protect it with all that we are. All creatures, orc, elf or man can call this land home. The Western Isles will be open to all."

The queen smiled, her expression one of genuine warmth. "Then go, my friends, and make your mark upon this land. May it flourish under your stewardship."

With the queen's words still echoing in their minds, Nagar and Irma turned their gaze westward, toward the rolling hills and lush valleys that would soon be their home. The journey to their new castle was one of quiet reflection, the landscape unfolding before them like a tapestry of promise. The castle itself stood atop a verdant hillside, overlooking a vast ocean, its stone walls gleaming in the sunlight, its towers reaching toward the heavens as if in silent prayer. It was a place of grandeur and serenity, a sanctuary from the storms of the past.

As they approached the castle, Nagar's eyes were drawn to Irma, his heart swelling with a love that seemed to grow deeper with each passing moment. Her smooth beige skin seemed to glow in the sunlight, her almond-shaped eyes reflecting the world around her with a quiet intensity. She was his strength, his anchor, and his joy, and in this moment, he felt a profound gratitude for the life they had built together.

He reached out, his hand gently taking hers, and pulled her close. His arms wrapped around her, his embrace warm and secure. "Irma," he whispered, his voice thick with emotion. "This place, this life—it's all because of you. I love you more than words can express."

Irma's lips curved into a soft smile, her hand rising to touch his cheek. "And I love you, Nagar. Together, we've faced the darkest of times, and yet here we are, standing at the threshold of a new beginning. This castle, this land—it's ours to shape, to fill with love and life."

Nagar's grin widened, his heart light with anticipation. "Then let us break this new home in properly. What do you say, my lady?"

Irma's eyes sparkled with mischief, her voice low and inviting. "I have just the idea in mind."

She led him through the grand halls of the castle, the air thick with the scent of fresh wood and stone. The tapestries that adorned the walls told stories of heroes and legends, their colors vibrant and rich. The sunlight streamed through the tall windows, casting long shadows that danced across the polished floors. It was a place of beauty and history, a place that felt both ancient and new.

At last, they reached the bedroom, a chamber of opulence and comfort. The bed, draped in silks and furs, seemed to beckon them, a promise of rest and passion. Irma turned to Nagar, her expression one of unspoken desire. "This is where we begin. This is where we start out family," she said, her voice barely above a whisper.

Nagar's heart raced as he took her in his arms, his lips finding hers in a kiss that was both tender and fierce. It was a kiss that spoke of love and longing, of the battles they had fought and the victories they had won. Their bodies moved in perfect harmony, each touch, each caress, a testament to the depth of their connection.

The world outside seemed to fade away as they surrendered to each other, their love igniting like a flame in the darkness. The passion between them was raw and unbridled, a force that seemed to consume them both. Nagar's hands traced the curves of Irma's body, his touch reverent and adoring. Irma's fingers tangled in his hair, her kisses hungry and desperate.

In that moment, there was only them, only the love that bound them together. The past, with all its pain and struggle, seemed distant and irrelevant. The future, with all its promise and uncertainty, was a blank canvas waiting to be filled. Here, in this room, in this castle, they were free to be themselves, to love without reservation, to live without fear.

When at last they lay entwined, their bodies glistening with sweat, their hearts still racing, Nagar pulled Irma close, his arm draped protectively around her. "I love you," he whispered, his voice hoarse with emotion.

Irma's fingers traced patterns on his chest, her smile soft and content. "And I love you, Nagar. Always and forever."

The days that followed were a blur of activity and discovery. Nagar and Irma explored their new domain, walking the lands that stretched as far as the eye could see. The Western Isles were a tapestry of rolling hills, dense forests, and a sparkling beach, each vista more breathtaking than the last. The air was crisp and clean, carrying the scent of the ocean breeze and earth, a stark contrast to the smoke and blood of the battlefield.

The castle itself was a marvel, its architecture a blend of strength and elegance. The great hall, with its vaulted ceiling and towering fireplaces, was a place of warmth and welcome. The library, with its shelves lined with ancient tomes and scrolls, was a sanctuary of knowledge and wisdom. The gardens, with their vibrant flowers and tranquil fountains, were a haven of peace and beauty.

As they walked the grounds, Nagar and Irma felt a sense of belonging, as if the land itself had been waiting for them. The people of the Western Isles, once wary and uncertain, soon came to see their new lords as protectors and providers. Nagar's fairness and Irma's compassion earned them the love and respect of their subjects, and the land began to flourish under their care.

But amidst the duties of governance and the joys of exploration, Nagar and Irma never forgot the love that had brought them to this place. Each night, as the sun dipped below the horizon and the stars began to twinkle in the sky, they would retreat to their chamber, a sanctuary of intimacy and passion. Their love was a constant, a flame that burned brightly no matter the challenges they faced.

One evening, as they sat by the fireplace in their chamber, the flames casting a warm glow over the room, Nagar turned to Irma, his expression thoughtful. "Do you ever think about the journey that brought us here?" he asked, his voice soft and reflective.

Irma smiled, her eyes meeting his. "Often. It's been a long road, filled with trials and triumphs. But every step, every sacrifice, has led us to this moment. I wouldn't change a thing."

Nagar reached out, his hand taking hers. "Neither would I. We've faced the darkness together, and together, we've found the light. This life, this love—it's more than I ever dreamed possible."

Irma leaned into him, her head resting on his shoulder. "It's a gift, Nagar. A gift we've earned through our struggles, our sacrifices. And now, it's ours to cherish, to protect, to celebrate."

Nagar's arm tightened around her, his heart full to bursting. "Then let us celebrate, my love. Let us make this life everything it can be, and more."

And so, they did. Each day was a celebration of their love, their resilience, their shared dream. They built a home that was a testament to their bond, a place where love and laughter filled the air, where the past was a memory and the future was a promise.

The Western Isles thrived under their care, the land blooming with life and prosperity. The people looked up to Nagar and Irma not just as their lords, but as symbols of hope and unity. The castle by the sea became a beacon, a place where all were welcome, where the ideals of justice and equality were lived and breathed.

And through it all, Nagar and Irma's love remained the heart of it all, a flame that burned brightly, illuminating the world around them. Their story, a tale of love and resilience, became a legend, whispered by the winds and sung by the rivers. It was a story of two souls who had faced the darkness together and emerged into the light, their love a guiding star for all who followed.

In the end, as they stood on the hillside, looking out over the land they had come to call home, Nagar turned to Irma, his heart full of gratitude and love. "This is our beginning," he said, his voice steady and sure. "Together, we've built a life worth living, a love worth fighting for. And together, we'll face whatever comes next."

Irma smiled, her eyes shining with tears of joy. "Together, always. No matter what the future holds, we'll face it side by side, hand in hand, heart to heart."

And as the sun dipped below the horizon, casting the sky in hues of gold and crimson, Nagar and Irma stood together, their love a beacon in the gathering dusk, a promise of a future filled with hope, joy, and endless possibility.

Don't miss out!

Visit the website below and you can sign up to receive emails whenever Matthew Gage publishes a new book. There's no charge and no obligation.

https://books2read.com/r/B-A-QBFOD-WCBEG

BOOKS 2 READ

Connecting independent readers to independent writers.

Did you love *The Sell Sword and The Elf*? Then you should read *The Power Couple*[1] by Matthew Gage!

New York City trembled, but Max Johnson, the invincible hero soaring through the skies, and Kira Yamamoto, the swift and regenerative samurai, stood as its unwavering protectors. Their partnership was forged in the heat of battle, their friendship tempered by shared victories. Max, with his flight, super-strength, and invulnerability, and Kira, a master of martial arts with the power to heal, were an unstoppable force.

But when a desperate plea from a besieged nation sends them across international borders, they cross a line, risking everything to save lives. Max, witnessing Kira's unwavering loyalty and courage, realizes their bond runs deeper than he ever imagined. The strength in her eyes, the

---

1. https://books2read.com/u/499MaW

2. https://books2read.com/u/499MaW

steel in her resolve, ignites a fire within him, a longing that transcends friendship.

High above the city lights, amidst the clouds they command, a stolen moment of passion erupts, a testament to the undeniable connection between them. As their romance blossoms, Max and Kira must navigate the complexities of their newfound feelings while facing the consequences of their actions. Can their love survive the scrutiny of a world they've defied, or will the weight of their heroic burdens keep their skybound hearts forever grounded?

Also by Matthew Gage

The Power Couple
The Sell Sword and The Elf

About the Author

Matthew Gage is a fantasy and Sci-Fi romance author writing about action, adventure and of course romance. He loves watching comic book movies and tv shows, reading comic books, and playing video games if he has time. He also writes interracial contemporary and historical romance under his pen name, Michael Gordon. Check out all of his books under the MG Publishing umbrella!

About the Publisher

MG Books is the publisher of the pen names of Michael Gordon and Matthew Gage. If you are a fan of Sci-Fi and fantasy romance, check out Matthew Gage's books. If you prefer more grounded contemporary romance, check out Michael Gordon's books.